spliffs 3

THE LAST WORD   IN CANNABIS CULTURE ?

spl ffs 3

THE LAST WORD   IN CANNABIS CULTURE ?

COLLINS & BROWN

First published in 2005 by Collins & Brown

An imprint of Chrysalis Books Group plc

The Chrysalis Building, Bramley Road, London W10 6SP, United Kingdom

An imprint of **Chrysalis** Books Group

© 2005 Chrysalis Books Group plc

ISBN: 1-84340-310-2

Text © Tim Pilcher

Volume © Chrysalis Books Group plc 2005

Commissioning editor: Chris Stone

Editor: Andy Nicolson

Designer: Rod Teasdale

Colour reproduction: Anorax

Printed and bound in Hong Kong by Imago

Additional text by Michelle Guilford and Rob Tribe

The Publishers would like to thank

Contents

Introduction

It's said that a week in politics is a long time. If that's the case, then a year in pot politics seems like a lifetime.

Since *Spliffs 2* came out, the UK has seen the government flip a massive 180° over its downgrading of cannabis from a Class B to a Class C drug. When the government finally announced in January 2004 that it had downgraded the drug it received a mixed, but generally positive, reception. It was seen as the Labour government's progressive approach to deal with an archaic and outmoded law.

But it wasn't long before the rot set in. Critics on both sides of the legalization argument warned that it sent a confusing message to Britain's youth, with the vast majority now believing that skinning up a joint was perfectly legal (which it isn't, kids!).

Then studies hinted that smoking cannabis allegedly doubles the risk of developing mental illnesses such as paranoia and schizophrenia in very heavy users aged under 18. This was enough for the right wing tabloids to start stirring up the old scaremonger stories that hadn't been heard since the days of William Randolph Hearst's propaganda war against marijuana back in the 1920s. Headlines like, "Addiction that made a teenager a killer," claiming that a 16 year old murdered his girlfriend because he'd smoked, "up to 600 cannabis joints a week."

It seemed that dope was back at the top of the media's agenda, with everyone wanting to cash in on the latest subject du jour. Even the relatively conservative *Woman's Hour* on BBC Radio 4 had a discussion about marijuana smoking amongst middle aged, middle class women. The debate ranged from over the top scaremongering by mental health charity SANE's Chief Executive, Marjorie Wallace, to a reasoned counterargument by consultant psychologist Dr Zerrin Attakan from the Maudsley Trust. Dr Attakan postulated that large amounts of THC may cause psychosis in younger, heavier smokers, but there needs to be more research into another cannabinoid, CBD, which appears to counter the effects of paranoia caused by excessive THC. Perhaps responsible growers and dealers will begin to reduce the levels of THC in their grasses and raise the level of CBD in future strains.

All of this culminated on the last day of the 2005 General Election campaign, when Prime Minister Tony Blair hinted at a possible U-turn, "We have asked for advice on it," he said. "What we did was perfectly sensible but I think it sent out the wrong message." What the right message is, is anybody's guess. That it's still illegal to grow certain plants? That it's OK to smoke some plants but not others? Or that it's OK to smoke whatever you like as long as you don't drive a car or hassle anyone while stoned? With all the new claims and counterclaims it seems as if the waters of cannabis legalization have become even more muddied. And I haven't even started on the medical marijuana argument! But I don't need to.

Inside, you'll find a whole chapter delving into the pros and cons of using cannabis for all sorts of medical conditions. Plus, there's information on how fantastic cannabis is, even if you don't smoke it, in Heavenly Hemp. Not forgetting a whirlwind historical tour of some of the best pro-pot festivals around the world. And to lighten the tone, there's a fun look at sensimilla on the silver screen, and a peek into the world of rolling paper collecting in Skins and Things.

The sub title of this book is "The last word in Cannabis Culture?" The way things are developing, I think we're only just beginning to start the real dialogue... In a year's time who knows where the discussion will be?

Tim Pilcher, Brighton, September 2005

Chapter 1

Sacred Herb

Across the globe and throughout history, cannabis has been used as a sacrament, either to enhance religious experience or as a deity in itself. The world's most ancient smokers and today's modern tokers continually refer to feelings of unity with God, peace, and a connection beyond the self, inspired by the use of marijuana.

Sacred Herb

Cannabis was used as an incense by the ancient Jews in the temples of Assyria and Babylon because its aroma was reputedly pleasing to the gods. Tens of thousands would gather for Friday night worship within a fragrant cloud of Kanabosom (marijuana) smoke, and then return home to the feast of the week with inspired appetites. Participants in an ancient tribal ceremony in the Zambezi Valley in Africa inhaled marijuana from a smouldering pile during worship. The 'barbaric' horsemen of the Scythians – in the Fifth century BC – also bathed themselves in sacred smoke as part of their rituals of the dead, "The Scythians, transported by the vapour, shout aloud," wrote Herodotus in 450 BC.

The Thracians of south east Europe burnt cannabis along with other psychoactive plants to create a mystical incense, which sent their sorcerers into trance. Known as 'Those who walk on smoke', these magicians were believed to have the power to transmute the cannabis vapours within them back into the plant, enabling them to directly embody its divine nature. The ancient Chinese also used cannabis. A Fifth century Taoist priest described how Chinese necromancers used the drug in combination with ginseng, "to set time forward and reveal future events."

Cannabis was also supposed to have been used as an anointing oil in some religions, notably Christianity, and possibly even by Jesus himself. Not surprising, when you contemplate the likelihood that at least one of the three wise men who journeyed to Bethlehem was a Zoroastrian. This Persian religion – which began around the Seventh century BC and is still alive today – is believed to hold cannabis as the chief sacrament of its priest class and its most important medicine. Hemp takes the prime position in the sacred text, the Avesta, which lists over 10,000 medicinal plants – surely the perfect gift for the Son of God.

Right: African pot puffing pygmies use it to get in touch with nature.

Spliffs 3

The ambitious claim that Jesus Christ was a dopehead derives from a mysterious ingredient in the saviour's famous, and liberally used, anointing oil. A passionate and high-faluting debate involving etymology, sociology, theology and medical properties, currently rages amongst cannabis devotees and Christians to try to ascertain just what "fragrant cane" God was referring to when he downloaded his recipe for "the holy anointing oil" to Moses (*Exodus 30: 22-25*).

Below: Don't Bogart that joint. Kids in a Coptic Church partake of the sacrament.

Traditionally thought to be the aromatic calamus, closer investigation has recently revealed that the "fragrant cane" was possibly cannabis. Not only does the Hebrew word 'Kanabosom' sound very much like cannabis, its root word 'kan', meaning either hemp or reed, is found in many ancient languages. Further examinations of Jesus' miraculous healings – performed with his potent oil – reveal that medically, there is a missing ingredient if one opts for calamus rather than cannabis. Within Judaic culture, cannabis was readily available and had a long association with healing uses, and nowhere in the Bible is it banned or criticized. Rather, God felt pretty good about all the plants he created and specifically praised "every herb bearing seed" (*Genesis 1:29*). Instructions were even given to, "Harvest, when the bud is perfect, and the sour grape is ripening in the flower." (*Isaiah 18:4-5*).

God's recipe for his son's holy anointing oil contained a blend of different spices including 5670g of myrrh (*commiphora myrrha*), 2835g of cinnamon (*cinnamomum zeylanicum*), 2835g of cannabis (*cannabis sativa*), 5670g cassia (*cassia ancienne/acacia farnesiana*) and a base of 3.8l of olive oil.

All that anyone with a Messiah complex has to do, is carefully blend these spices and oil in a dark glassed bottle and shake vigorously. Check for any allergic reaction and if it's all clear, a small amount may be used to anoint the brow for ritual purposes.

Rasta

Rastafarianism is a grassroots revolutionary religion with followers worldwide and 'wisdom weed' at its heart. Their Jesus is not only dope wielding but black too, as is Adam. God is known as 'Jah' and the Bible is the Holy Piby or 'the black man's bible.' Smoking is central to the tradition of most Rastas, as a way of coming closer to Jah and achieving the mystical union of 'I and I.' According to Rastas, ganja, also known

Above: A Rastafarian prepares to talk with Jah, by smoking a chalice of weed.

"The issue here is not marijuana. Marijuana is the messenger, not the message. The issue is whether we will live in freedom or under tyranny. The most basic of all human rights is the right to your own body. The lighted marijuana weed is the torch of freedom."

Dr. Julian Heicklen, Emeritus Professor of Chemistry, Pennsylvania State University, 26 September 1998.

"It is certainly no longer true to say – if it ever was – that smoking cannabis is a sign of affiliation to an 'alternative' lifestyle. Clearly, in the light of its popularity, and to a degree its apparent social acceptability, questions are raised about the legalization of cannabis."

The Misuse of Drugs report, Office of Health Economics (UK).

Above: A Jamaican 'Yardie' enjoys the heavenly herb in Kingston town.

as 'charge', is apparently the "green herb" referred to in the King James Bible and also, "the herb of the field" which Jah commands his followers to use in the book of Genesis (3:18) "for the service of man" (*Psalms 104:14*).

According to Rastafarian tradition, the sacred herb helps the oppressed to open their hearts and reconnect with their native African heritage, and it forms part of an ideology of inner peace, I-tal (pure) vegetarianism, and a return to nature.

"The Rasta sees ganja as part of his religious observance" said leading Rastafarian Sam Brown. Apparently it first grew on the grave of King Solomon, the wisest man on earth. It balances the mind and creates a peaceful contemplative state suitable for meditation and 'reasoning', which is central to Rasta worship and is characteristically informal. A group of 'brethren' gather, often in the street, and one of the elders present will be honoured with lighting the chalice and reciting a short prayer whilst the others bow their heads, "Glory be to Father and to the maker of creation. As it was in the beginning, is now and ever shall be. World without end: Jah Rastafari: Eternal God Selassie-I". Once the chalice is lit, the elder will take several long pulls and inhale deeply, entering a trance like state. He repeats this two or three times and then passes the pipe anti-clockwise round the circle until all the brothers have toked.

Whilst 'reasoning' is a chance for Rastas to talk and reflect, the 'nyabinghi' are ceremonial celebrations which often last several days. They generally fall on important dates from Rasta history – the most auspicious being the coronation of His Imperial Majesty (HIM), the Ethiopian prince Ras Tafari Makonnen, who became Emperor on November 2, 1930. The crowning of Ras Tafari fulfilled the prophecy of black activist Marcus Garvey, who wanted to unite the blacks with their homeland and told the people in the 1920s to, "Look to Africa for the crowning of a king to know that your redemption is near." The Emperor gave himself the humble title of Haile Selassie (Power of the Trinity) and simultaneously became inaugurated in the consciousness of many Jamaican blacks as a divine embodiment of Jah, sent to redeem them from Babylonian (white) suppression and supremacy.

Above: As reggae rocked the world, Rastafarianism and reefer rolled with it.

During 'nyabinghi' celebrations, hundreds of Rastas from all over Jamaica camp around a specially built tabernacle. Formal evening smoking and dancing gives way to an orgy of music into the early hours, and the days are spent lulling in 'rest and reason'.

Personal Highs:

"I saw God, man…"

In 1989, Hong Kong writer Shellie Wong and her artist brother stayed on Cheung Chau Island, to get creative inspiration. A little experimental cooking was thrown into the mix one evening, bringing on the trip of a lifetime.

"I had been smoking dope for a few years before I finally ate some; a night not to be forgotten! I crumbled some kind of hash into my brownie mixture, tasted the batter, baked it, tried a slice then tidied up the tray by eating the crumbs. I then had two more slices with my brother and some girl he had met. It was a balmy summer evening and all was well…

"We passed the next hour eating and chatting, watching the moon rise over the sea. My brother then decided it was time to put on my Dad's nylon 70s' dressing gown and slippers to walk his date home. Whilst they were gone, I started to buzz and vibrate. Everything in the room around me started to move. I poured a glass of water and decided it was time to lie down.

"Then the tripping began. With each breath, the experience became more intense until I was in a vortex of movement. The sound and rhythm of my breath, the swirling colours behind my closed eyes… taking me higher and higher as if each part of my body was being pulled into a single hypnotic rhythm, which was literally drawing me out of my flesh. Every now and then

I would land back in my bed, pulled there by a crazy thirst. I would reach thankfully for the glass of water, but as soon as the liquid hit the ball of chocolate coated dope in my stomach, there was a mad chemical reaction, masses of THC were instantly released into my bloodstream and I spun off again, each time further and further away from consciousness.

"I became aware that I was filled with huge amounts of psychotropic cake, and that I had to choose between two overwhelming experiences; either tortuous thirst or freaky tripping. If I drank, aaahh! Thirst for a moment quenched – then wooooow! Off again to the outer reaches of the energetic universe only to land back in bed once the thirst returned.

"It was on one of these trips that I arrived in a place I can only describe as heaven - the most beautiful landscape of grass and distant trees… The sky was a huge paisley, the stillness absolute and I was in a state of great empathic connection. If I looked at the grass, I became the grass. I could feel everything of what it was to be a blade of grass, the ecstatic feeling of pushing through the earth, the utter physical joy of bending in the wind – the absolute compression of being, which comes when each moment is purely experienced without the filter of mental consciousness.

"When I looked at the trees it was the same – I became them. I could become the sky too, each feeling slightly different, and yet each one also coloured by the same feelings of ecstatic joy and an almost orgasmic connection.

"As I looked, I realised that the only experience greater than this was to experience everything in the glowing scene at the same time. Not only to become the essence of the grass and then the trees and then the sky, but to become grass, trees and sky all at once. Perhaps I need to eat a little more next time.

"'Are you all right?' My brother stuck his head around the bedroom door. 'I've just had the maddest trip!' I exclaimed, sitting up. 'Me too,' he giggled, pulling the brown nylon dressing gown around him, 'Me too.'"

Whether it's right or Wong, a pure cannabis high can't be beaten if it's eaten.

"With each breath, the experience became more intense until I was in a vortex of movement."

Marijuana itself is sacred, their 'Iley' is central to the religion. It is seldom smoked recreationally by true Rastas – that would be sacrilege. Instead, it is used to aid revelation of the divine within and the true Godhead of Haile Selassie. Rastas believe that the average Jamaican is so brainwashed by colonialism and the corruption of Babylon, that he needs a helping spliff to see the wood from the trees. By smoking and reasoning, the Rasta encounters his true self, has a true revelation of black consciousness and a proper love of the black race and, most importantly, knows that Haile Selassie is God and Ethiopia the true home of the blacks. This is what Bob Marley was referring to when he

Below: Rastas relax to 'rest and reason'. Or 'get stoned', as it's known elsewhere.

exhorted his people to, "Emancipate yourselves from mental slavery / None but ourselves can free our minds." To the Rasta, God is both within and without, hiding away in their corrupted consciousnesses and existing in the cosmic realm in the form of Jah. The intermediary, the personification of God on Earth, is Haile Selassie, and their greatest tool for accessing all these sacred manifestations is 'the holy herb'.

Ras Sam Clayton summed up the significance of marijuana to Rastas in a 1975 interview, "Man, basically, is God, but this insight can come to man only with the use of the herb. When you use the herb, you experience yourself as God. With the use of the herb you can exit this dismal state of reality that exists in Jamaica. You cannot change man, but you can change yourself by the use of the herb. When you are God you deal with or relate to people like a God. In this way you let your light shine, and when each of us lets his light shine we are creating a God like culture, and this is the cosmic unity that we try to achieve in the Rastafarian community."

Shinto

On the other side of the world, a very different religion is linked to Rastafarianism by a shared love of weed. Shintoism – Japan's indigenous religion – celebrates hemp as a symbol of spiritual purity and uses it as a tool of purification. A nature based religion with ancestor worship beyond the grave, there is little smoke on this path, rather a reverence for the plant itself and a range of spiritually significant, practical uses of the fibre.

In old traditions, rice, salt and hemp were the staple offerings to Kami, or the divine – including various gods and deities – at Shinto shrines or jinja. The shrines' thick bell ropes must be made from hemp fibre, as must the noren, a purification veil which people pass under to rid their bodies of evil spirits. To complete the ritual of cleansing, the Shinto priest would then shake a gohei wand of hemp fibres over the heads of the worshippers wearing – yes, you guessed it – starched hemp paper robes. As in the Shinto marital chamber, hemp fibre represents the ultimate purity with the power to dissolve any darkness or demons. Always included in a dowry, undyed hemp fabric is important in the household of a new Shinto bride. It symbolizes her faithfulness, chastity and obedience and, like the un-dyed cloth, the woman is a pure material ready to be 'coloured' by her husband.

Hemp is also key to the Imperial family, who are regarded as descendants of the Shinto gods. In 1989, the long reigning Emperor Hirohito finally died. Since he came to power, hemp growing had become effectively illegal (1948) thanks to the occupying Americans, so there was no obvious source for the new Emperor's hemp clothes. Luckily, a group of farmers with foresight in Tokushima-Ken had bravely planted a crop for just this purpose and they were able to present the new Emperor with his vital hemp robes.

Hemp is still grown for the Imperial family at this site, and very fine cloths and papers are still produced in parts of Japan, but the application process for a license to grow hemp is frustratingly lengthy and often futile.

Special strategies have had to be employed to make sure that the Shinto religion is still able to use its sacred plant for symbolic purposes. Small plantations exist in Japan to supply the temples with their bell ropes, curtains and other hemp essentials, and the Japanese tourist board still includes hemp as part of its cultural colour, reminding visitors not to miss the annual lion dance in honour of the god who brought hemp and cotton to the land. With hemp as a central Shinto symbol of purity, it seems ironic that Japan takes a particularly harsh line on more modern uses of cannabis . Users are called 'happachu' or 'happaboke', phrases which mean 'weed junkie' and which also describe users of heroine and cocaine, obviously alluding to great impurity.

Sufi

Meanwhile, back in the Middle East, the Sufis, a heretical sect existing on the fringes of Islam, were using kaif. Cannabis historian Ernest Abel described these mystical priests as, "The hippies of the Arab world." To the Sufis, cannabis or kaif was sacred, and was used to excite mystical consciousness, divine revelation, insight and oneness with Allah. The story goes that the leader of one Persian Sufi tradition, called Haidar, was wandering in the mountains one day in the 12th century when he happened upon a cannabis plant. As the day was hot, he rested beneath the plant, nibbling on a few leaves as he cooled down and chilled out, and thus unwittingly performed the first Sufi act of worship of its kind. On his return to the monastery, his disciples were so impressed with their usually down in the mouth leader's happy and communicative demeanour, that they promptly went out and tried the plant for themselves. The result was so good that kannab was inaugurated at the centre of Sufi religious practice, permitting, as Sufi al'Is'irdi noted, "the spirit to ascend to the highest points in a heavenly ascension of disembodied understanding."

The 'god intoxicated' Sufis moved on from their miserable mystic predecessors (known as 'those who always weep') by bringing mahabba (love) and ma'joun (chewy cannabis pulverized with honey) to their religious practices. Guided by the spirit of their sacred herb, the Sufis follow the Qu'ran but abandon the cerebral theology of Islam, instead believing that God can only be reached through personal experience and direct vision. Through dhikr (ritual prayers), repetitious chanting, silent meditation, the dance of the whirling dervishes, and even sama sessions with music and poetry, the Sufi enters a drug enhanced ecstatic experience of intoxication. For the sober mystics amongst them, coffee rather than cannabis

Left: There's nothing like a blast from a hookah full of hash for "heavenly ascension".

Above: While Sufis smoke sensi, Muslims decline marijuana, and stick to apple tobacco.

is the drug of choice, enabling them to stay up for night long vigils of prayer, devotion and twahid – asserting oneness with God.

The Sufi tradition survives to this day, although prohibition in many areas of the Middle East makes explicit use of their sacred drug increasingly difficult. Many modern Muslims criticize the peacenik Sufis for being escapist and avoiding taking up Jihads. However, the Sufis have proved themselves to be very successful missionaries with global followers, even in countries such as Turkey where mystical orders have been banned since 1925, and at The High Sufi Convent in Egypt. There are at least 60 Sufi religious orders around the world today.

Art influenced by marijuana

Cannabis inspired art has a diverse and colourful history. From paintings of the Buddha holding his daily dose of a single hemp seed, to the slightly satanic self portrait of the infamous dopehead of the *Club des Haschines*, Charles Baudelaire, artists across the world and throughout time have found inspiration in *cannabis sativa*.

There are many fine paintings of domestic hemp production scenes, from primitive Chinese hemp paper making to Augustus Atkinson's 1804 painting of Russian women and children sorting and drying hemp. There are botanical drawings and woodcuts of *cannabis sativa* in many old herbals, and images of peaceful smoking sessions from 19th century India.

And of course, there are paintings borne of the drug experience itself. Characteristically complex and interlaced, one fine example of this reefer randomness is Jean-Martin Charot's crazed maze, painted in 19th century Paris. But *every* now and then a lucid work emerges, such as Horace Vernet's portrait of himself smoking 'hasheesh' in 1835. A delicate whorl of smoke curls from a long tapered pipe and a distinct aura emanates from the artist smoker's head, perhaps denoting his excited, creative mind. Above this however, is a dark smoky ceiling depicting either the gloom of normal consciousness lifting, or creative constriction about to close in.

Cannabis is widely celebrated as a creativity enhancer, and research by Miles Herkenham published in *Omni* magazine in 1989 supports this. The active cannabinoids, such as THC, mimic the molecular key, anandamide, allowing them to attach to 'bliss receptors' on nerve cells. But once the inspiration has struck, is the drug any good when actually putting pen or brush to paper?

"Marijuana unlocks the ability of my mind to think in new and creative ways," confessed one switched on San Francisco doctor. Artists report a deeper resonance with archetypes, reduced inhibition, and a keener eye for the subtleties of colour, tone and subject within an artwork. "Marijuana allows us to choose from an expanded palette of moods as our attention drifts through various levels of consciousness," one 47 year old artist observed.

There's a colourful collage of artists who draw inspiration from the weed. There are trippy 'toons – re-inventions of childhood favourites such as the red eyed, spliff wielding Drugs Bunny, and Alice in her wonderland with a bong smoking caterpillar on a 'shroom. Modern marijuana graffiti art also reflects great interest in getting high, while other 'sensitive' artists create

Above: Charles Baudelaire's druggy doodle, done while doped out.

self reflective, self referential journeys into the drug unlocked psyche. There are beautiful celebrations of the leaf and the bud, merging digital photography with botanical accuracy, and there are the far out journeys of metaphysical

Right: An intense Jean-Martin Charcot drawing, created under the influence of hashish.

artists who use the drug to access distant dimensions, resulting in images of divas, energy fields and the ecstatic expansion of the high. Others simply draw while off their nut.

And there is a whole art movement dedicated to the politics of pot. The Victorians produced many satanic images of marijuana monsters mauling simpering smokers, with others, more subtly executed but with the same underlying message, depicting scenes of 'Hasheesh Hell'. In the present day we have political art championing the hemp movement, with groups such as

SMART (Smoke & Art) and AHEMP (Artists Helping End Marijuana Prohibition) dedicated to utilizing the arts as a medium for re-educating the public about marijuana history and uses.

Most artists who smoke agree that weed does wonders for their inspiration. Many take notes and draw preliminary sketches whilst tripping. However, it seems that fine brushwork and absolute precision are more difficult while stoned. One London artist, musician and midnight toker, known as Colon Beach, confessed, "I have not found smoking weed particularly useful in creating artworks." He tried it at college but gave up, and puts his lack of success down to the nature of his work, "which is precise, rational and almost scientific in its attempt to test the subject matter." While trying to do some anatomical drawing stoned, he found he had, "a floaty head full of random musings… I just wanted to put the pencil down and go lie down in a field to watch the clouds."

The main obstacle to creating art while wasted, it appears, is too much inspiration. As Thomas Edison said, genius is 1% inspiration and 99% perspiration, and perspiration seems best supported by a sober rather than a stoned state. The danger of executing that dope inspired dreamscape whilst off with the faeires, is that it's likely to look like a whole lot of self indulgent crap in the cold light of day. And for this there is only one answer. As artist Colon Beach suggests, "Maybe the trick here is not to sober up…"

Alternatively, don't pick up a brush at all, but take a tip from Allen Ginsberg; get stoned and visit a gallery. The 'fine art, fine weed' cocktail apparently offers profound pontification and amazing aesthetic discoveries. Maybe art critics like Brian Sewell need to get stoned more often.

Left: Indian stoners mix up a big, bad bowl of bhang to get blasted on. Bhang can also make cookies, juices and cake.

While the idea of reaching an ecstatic oneness with God by dancing around chewing sacred cannabis cud with the loved up Sufis might be appealing to many Western spiritual seekers, do not forget that asceticism is at the heart of this religion. In other words, if you want to smoke the sacramental Sufi way, you've got to give up everything you own first. And yes, that includes your *Cheech and Chong* DVDs.

Sadhus

The wandering wise men of an old Hindu tradition – the Sadhus – are famous for their extreme acts of asceticism as well as for their appetite for the sacred ganja. Most are followers of Shiva, some are charlatans, but the vast majority will be seen brandishing charras packed chillums. Holy men who have taken vows of poverty and chastity, the Sadhus are known to stand for years on one leg, bury themselves in sand, sleep in piles of thorns, retreat for years to silence or mountain caves as signs of devotion. Many stoners have a similar devotion to their sofas.

Smoking will definitely soften the discomfort of the penances of the suffering Sadhu – their ganja is also called 'soother of grief' and 'poor man's heaven' – but there is more to it than this. Bhang, a milky cannabis cocktail, is used by the Sadhus to clear away evil influences (especially first thing in the morning), banish fear, prolong life, bless all desires, deepen and quicken thought by clearing ignorance, liberate 'self from self' and, most importantly, to make man one with the divine. As the 1894 Indian Hemp Drugs Commission reported, "In the ecstasy of bhang the spark of the Eternal in man turns into light the murkiness of matter or illusion, and self is lost in the central soul fire."

The smokin' Sadhus come from ancient Hindu traditions of marijuana use where it is a heavenly guide and 'skyflier', a truly holy plant in its own right. Hindu legends say that where amrita, or divine nectar of immortality, dropped from the heavens, there sprang up the sacred plant bhang – food of the gods. Another legend has it that when amrita was produced from the churning ocean, something was needed to purify the nectar. So Mahadev made bhang for the purpose from his own body, giving the plant the name angaj, meaning body born. Whichever story you tell, the moral is the same – bhang is deeply sacred, it contains the body and essence of the divine being of Mahadev/Shiva, and those who drink it come closer to siddha, or oneness with the deity.

Offerings of bhang are still made at Hindu temples in certain festivals, with different recipes for different deities. Very often it is poured onto Shiva's lingham (penis) and what is not used is sometimes fed to the sacred cows. Not only is the drinker of bhang promised fulfillment of all

Right: A sensi smoking Sadhu at the festival of Kumbh Mela, the world's largest religious gathering.

desires and deep spiritual connection, but those who refuse to smoke or sip bhang shall be, "cast into hell". Even more woe is promised to those who criticize ritual use of 'the joy giver' as they, "shall suffer the torments of hell so long as the sun endures". Indeed, "He who drinks wisely and according to rule, be he ever so low, even though his body is smeared with human odure and urine, is Shiva."

Above: In Indian mythology, Shiva is the discoverer, user and patron saint of pot.

The rules for smoking or drinking the sacred herb are relatively simple. Allen Ginsberg describes a Shivaist gathering before a shrine of flowers and sacramental milk candy, during which holy songs were sung all night to the divine spirit, and in which ganja was used as a part of sadhana – the process of evoking the deity within the plant and absorbing it into the self, "The great ganja pipe is packed and lit – 'Bom! Bom! Mahadev!' (Boom! Boom! Great God!) or 'Bom Shankar!' they cry, as the chillum or pipe is raised to the brows and then inhaled."

Buddhism

To say that all Buddhists are partial to puff would be wildly untrue, but there are sects, particularly in the mountain regions of Tibet and Nepal, for whom cannabis is a revered meditation aid and aphrodisiac.

One Mahayana legend states that Siddhartha used and ate nothing but hemp seeds during the six years prior to enlightenment and becoming the Buddha in the Fifth century BC, and more recently, we find a prized variety of potent hash in the Nepalese 'Temple Ball', which carries the tradition to the present day. The Buddhist monks would take the sacred bhang as a tea, as maajun candy or smoke charras rolled with tobacco to help them see through the smoke screen of worldly illusions (samsara) and thereby experience nirvana – release from the cycle of reincarnation and finally, realization of their latent Buddha nature.

Tantric Buddhism is a part of the Vajrayana tradition of esoteric Buddhism, which believes that liberation from samsara is more quickly reached through mystical sense pleasure. As an individual based, sense centred practice, this religion has a particularly strong relationship with cannabis. Tantrics use it as a protector and purifier to challenge the power of demons, and it is also incorporated into their meditation and sexual rites.

In the 'Kalacakra Tantra', the Buddha apparently says that enlightenment must be achieved through the body, which itself contains the whole universe. Many Tantric sutras, such as the Ghyasamaja Tantra, describe elaborate rituals which strongly sniff of group orgies, although some scholars try to wriggle out of this one by saying that the sexual bits represent a symbolic union of wisdom (female) and means (male). About an hour and a half before the ritual, devotees utter the mantra "Ohm hrim, O ambrosia formed goddess [Kali] who has arisen from ambrosia, who showers ambrosia, bring me ambrosia again and again, bestow occult power [siddhi] and bring my chosen deity to my power." They then drink a big bowl of bhang, and once it has taken effect, the ceremony takes off.

One ritual is called the chakrapuja and it goes as follows. Between eight and 48 men and women gather in a sacred space and drink some bhang as above. The priest anoints and then has intercourse with a naked young girl, retaining his semen for the congregation to drink. Feasting

Above: Worshippers of Kali, the Goddess of death and rebirth, also smoke weed.

and drinking follow and the ceremony ends with ritual copulation whilst reciting mantras. Having a good time is not the point, apparently. Rather, it's about using sexual union and orgasm to extinguish the self and fuse with the overlying

reality and Unity. A bhang-ing good time in every sense.

But the East doesn't have a monopoly on the use of wacky baccy in religious practices. Paganism has plenty of gods and goddesses and almost as many traditions, but common to all

Above: Chinese men in Xingjian Province get blasted on a big bamboo bong.

pagans is the pursuit of, "their own vision of their Divine as a direct and personal experience," according to the Pagan Federation UK. Within this magical nature religion, the use of herbs for healing and spiritual revelation are central. Although cannabis and hemp are not as well publicized as other potent (and sometimes poisonous) magical herbs, they play a part in many rituals and sacred brews. "Cannabis has been used for centuries as a sacred herb, allowing the magician to loosen the hold of the material world and gain access to the other realms. However, any relationship with a power plant is precarious, and its spirit must be approached with respect," wrote Susan Lavender and Anna Franklin in their book, *Herb Craft*.

According to the recipes of 17th century Italian physician Giovanni De Ninalut, cannabis was possibly an ingredient in mediaeval witches' famous psychedelic 'flying ointment', in combination with datura, aconite, parsnip, belladonna, cinqfoil and water, all stewed in fat. The result would be mixed with soot and then smeared over the body or else smeared onto the handle of a broomstick and inserted into the vagina. Whichever method was used, the result was a powerful hallucination akin to flying (on the broomstick of course), echoing the Hindu nickname for cannabis of 'skyflier'.

Entheobotanist Dr Christian Ratsch's study of ancient German texts linked a potent hemp 'beer' to fertility rites of the first millennium AD. Pagans

Right: A prehistoric pipe from America proves that stoners have been around longer than laws.

would gather at the spring equinox to celebrate the goddess Ostara (the root word and festival for our Easter) and, after its sacrifice and consumption, they would wash down their sacred animal, the hare, with a good hemp beer. No normal beer either. This brew was carefully concocted by wise women and hedge witches who would mix in all kinds of herbs including hemp and henbane, resulting in 'Bacchanalian orgies'.

Other goddess rites involving cannabis include innocent fertility rites dedicated to Freya, the Norse love goddess. Young girls would steal away to the hemp fields at night to make wreaths of hemp, which they would throw onto low

boughs whilst being watched by the local boys. This innocent ritual, drawing on cannabis as a love drug, was captured in the records of the Inquisition and deemed satanic. Another condemned ritual was the dance of some young hemp harvesters. They became so high on the fragrant aroma of the crop that they stripped off, only to be accused by the Inquisition of having an, "orgy with the devil".

So, the story of sacred sativa is a diverse and colourful one, and many themes and patterns can be traced through the rituals and practices of these and many other cannabis using faiths, past and present. According to most religions, weed is sacred to numerous gods and goddesses from Allah to Artemis and Shiva to Selassie, as a means of creating closer communication with the elusive world of spirit. Those traditions and sects which place people at the centre of their own individual spiritual faith are most partial to the inspiration which comes from smoking, smudging or sucking on the plant in one form or another. Religions which seek tighter control of their congregations and their political frameworks, and those for whom the universe beyond is filled with evil spirits and vindictive ancestors, demonise the weed and stick with formal ceremony and symbolic Eucharists – rather than taking a trip and going with the flow.

Left: This stone pipe was used for ceremonial smoking amongst prehistoric Native Americans.

Some believe that the holy herbs of early pagans and shamans evolved into the placebo sacraments of the modern Christian church. Others go even further to claim that the innocent eating of the hempen plant of pleasure – in the Eden like forests of the ancient world – actually gave rise to the first idea of a God to primitive Homo sapiens. Forbidden fruit indeed. Professor Richard E Schultes, Director of the Botanical Museum at the University of Harvard, and a prominent researcher of psychoactive plants wrote,

Above: In Nepal, hippies sought expanded consciousness by getting wasted.

"Upon eating hemp, the euphoric, ecstatic and hallucinatory aspects may have introduced man to an other worldly plane from which emerged religious beliefs, perhaps even the concept of a deity. The plant becomes accepted as a special gift of the gods, a sacred medium for communication with the spiritual world and as such, it has remained in some cultures to the present."

Chapter 2

Dope Dissent

Ever since Harry J Anslinger and his cronies at the Federal Bureau of Narcotics succeeded in convincing the US Government to ban cannabis in 1937, there's been resistance.

Dope Dissent

But the struggle has been long and hard, and for the first few years it all went in favour of the prohibitionists. As Anslinger testified to Congress that marijuana was the most violence causing drug known to man, the objections of the American Medical Association were simply ignored. In 1944, Anslinger sought revenge on those who dared to challenge his party line, and threatened doctors who carried out cannabis research with imprisonment. But four years later, the Head of the Federal Bureau of Narcotics (FBN) had completely changed his ideas about the demon weed, now stating that users were peaceful and that cannabis could be used during a communist invasion to weaken American will to fight. Consistency was never Anslinger's strong point.

His crowning glory was to be to get the UN to pass Treaty 406 – The Single Convention on Narcotic Drugs – to outlaw cannabis use and cannabis cultivation worldwide, with the plan to eradicate cannabis smoking within 30 years. Obviously, and thankfully, the old 'stick in the mud' failed and the following year, 1962, he was forcibly retired by private pot smoker, President Kennedy.

Early days

Amazingly, it took nearly 30 years for a real, coherent and vocal opposition to prohibition to coalesce. It wasn't until 1967 and the first 'Summer of love', when Steve Abrams' UK organisation, the Society Of Mental Awareness (SOMA) placed a full page advertisement in *The Times*, calling for reform of the law on cannabis. SOMA managed to get 65 leading figures in the arts – including The Beatles – and sciences and medicine to sign it. The advertisement declared the existing law, "immoral in principle and unworkable in practice." It was debated in the House of Commons, where the Minister of State, Alice Bacon, announced an expert inquiry headed by Baroness Wootton. In January 1969, the 'Wootton Report' on cannabis endorsed the position taken in the advertisement that, "the long asserted dangers of cannabis were exaggerated, and that the related law was socially

Right: John Lennon was an ardent campaigner for the legalization of cannabis.

damaging, if not unworkable." It was a major coup for campaigners, but was predictably ignored by the government.

But British tokers weren't to be defeated so easily. On 1 May, a date that would become intrinsically entwined with cannabis campaigning, 3,000 people held a 'smoke-in' at Speakers' Corner in Hyde Park. Then, two months later on 16 July, over 10,000 turned up again in Hyde Park for a pro-legalisation rally. The engine of dissent had been started.

Simultaneously in America, a young Dana Beal organized the first US marijuana protests. These mass 'smoke-ins' were the grass seeds of Beal's unrelenting, almost 40 year campaign to have cannabis legalized once more. Beal was a founding member of the Youth International Party. The 'Yippies', as they quickly became known, were essentially a political hippie fellowship. At the time, the mood in America was revolutionary, and many neo-political groups were springing up, such as Students for a Democratic Society (SDS), a loosely organized federation of 300 campus chapters. The SDS leaders included Tom Hayden, who went on to marry marijuana smoking actress and Sixties' icon, Jane Fonda. All of the groups shared a common hatred of the Vietnam War, and a resentment and distrust of the political system. Judging by society's mood today, very little has changed. Simply substitute Iraq for Vietnam.

The Yippies were a coalition 'led' by Jerry Rubin and Abbie Hoffman, along with others, including Dana Beal. Rubin was best known for dressing in a revolutionary terrorist outfit and blowing bubbles at an Un-American Activities Committee hearing. Many groups in the Sixties were so earnest and self righteous that the Yippies provided rare comedic relief amongst the radicals. "The Yippies are anything you want them to be," grinned Hoffman in 1968. "They're a myth." Hoffman, like Rubin, believed in a vague, anarchist future with no central government and no currency. Just one big happy commune with free goods and services.

One of the Yippies' first stunts was at the New York Stock Exchange, when they floated down dollar bills and then laughed hysterically as millionaire stockbrokers scrambled madly after the money. They simultaneously celebrated the 'death of money' and exposed America's greedy society. One of the Sixties' survivors, Michael Forman, ruminated in 2003 how the playing field for the Yippies' brand of mischief had changed, "If we dropped dollar bills at the Stock Exchange now," he said, "it would be perceived as a terrorist act."

Throughout the Sixties, the Yippies committed numerous 'terrorist acts' as they plastered 'See Canada Now' signs on US Army recruiting booths, and famously mailed 3,000 marijuana joints to random strangers in the phone book. As the Yippies gained more attention however, the

Right: Jerry Rubin decided on formal dress for the hearings in 1969.

How to be a dope smuggler

You and I may be guilty of bringing the odd blim or unfinished baggie back home after a weekend in Amsterdam, but that's nothing compared to shifting tons of high grade Mary Jane around the world. Here's what you should know if you fancy a career change.

First, get to know a huge rock band. Howard Marks, one of the UK's most prolific former marijuana smugglers, and an advocate for its legalization, used this technique to supply America with some great quality spliff. With the help of some of the major bands of the day, Marks moved 30 tons of the stuff across international borders. The constant stream of bands coming from the UK to conquer the US music market provided ample opportunity to stash the hash in numerous speaker cabinets. Groups such as Genesis, Eric Clapton, Emerson Lake and Palmer, and Pink Floyd unwittingly helped shift tons of hash and grass around the world.

Next, you need an alias or two. During his career as an international dope smuggler, Marks notched up 43 aliases, had nearly 90 different phone lines, and traded under 25 company names. Aliases included the infamous Mr Nice, D

H Marks, Senor Marco and Marco Polo… not the most inventive names perhaps, so use your imagination. Avoid monikers like Mr Cheech, Mr Chong or Spliffy McSpliffster!

Alternatively, you could join the US Navy. Being a member of America's armed services is not just an excuse to ride roughshod over foreign nations, it is an excellent way to smuggle hashish. Allegedly, one frequently utilized method is to ship the stuff around on aircraft carriers. These things are big, and can be home to up to 5,000 people. A person in a position of power on one of those things can make use of numerous storage facilities on board, most obviously the lifeboats. No one messes with these things – people's lives may depend on them – and their containers have ample space for a couple of kilos stashed away here and there. Load up in Hawaii, unload in San Diego. Remember, an army marches on its stomach – especially when it's got the munchies.

And it's important to be flexible and to use every resource available. Everyone's heard of cars' sills packed with bricks of weed, or dope drops made by plane, but in Canada (a country fast becoming a trailblazer in cannabis production) the sea is the ultimate method. From fake whales to disguising your contraband as floating kelp, the chance to earn $1,000 in an afternoon if you know anything about the sea, is being seized upon by many a dope smuggler. Savvy contra-bandits even created remote control logs, hollowed out to carry wacky baccy,

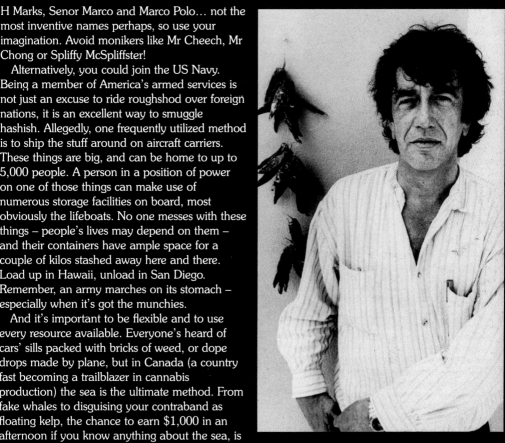

Above: Howard Marks' autobiography, *Mr Nice*, is a "How to…" guide for aspiring smugglers.

and then 'floated' them towards a logging operation, where they were picked up by unsuspecting workers, loaded on to trucks, and then picked up again by the smugglers after reaching their destination. Techno-log-y at work!

It's good to have friends in the smuggling business, and some of the best are the CIA. You may not have heard of Operations Snow Cone, Toilet Seat or Whale Watch, but all of them were alleged CIA drug smuggling operations. Operation Toilet Seat involved flying the drugs out of South America in Boeing 727s and dumping them out of the back in waterproof containers to be picked up by boat and taken to US shores. Operation Whale Watch meanwhile,

Below: Dope addicted sniffer dogs corner a cannabis courier at the US border.

used off shore oil rigs as a cover for smuggling drugs, flying them by helicopter from the rigs to the US. There are even rumours of Operation Watchtower; a secret network of radio beacons that allow CIA pilots to make drug runs at low altitude to avoid radar detection.

Of course, if you are flying the plane yourself, make sure you know where you're going. Tom Forcade, the journalist behind *High Times* magazine, and renowned dope smuggler, was once flying a load around Mexico when he got lost. Eventually, he spotted the fires of a private landing strip and touched down. However, "It was some other smuggler's landing strip. They were quite upset… they were expecting another type of plane, a different person, a different code word and everything. I had trouble explaining myself. And I was out of gas."

If you are serious about taking up this lucrative career, you should also prepare to spend the rest of your life in jail, as some countries will simply lock you up and throw away the key for smuggling small quantities of dope. Remember, the film *Midnight Express* was based a true story! However, some countries won't waste the precious resources needed for a life sentence on a foreigner, and will just execute you. You have been warned…

Right: As a marijuana smuggler, the customs officer is not your friend!

focus shifted towards pulling off even more outrageous activities, rather than setting up 'counter institutions' like the Free Store for the poor in New York. Some began to accuse the Yippies of provoking violent confrontations with the police, and vice versa.

At midnight on 22 March 1968, the Yippies held an all night party at Grand Central Station, New York – a location they considered to be the hub of the bourgeoisie's 9-to-5 working life. Word got out that they were celebrating the spring equinox and 6,000 people turned up. Some frolicked with balloons while others shouted militant slogans and set off bangers. The cops quickly crashed the party, beating people with sticks as the crowd shouted, "Sieg heil!"

Everything culminated later that year at the 1968 Democratic Convention in Chicago. The Yippies put forward a pig as their candidate for President, highlighting the poor choice of humans, and threatened to slip LSD into the Chicago water system, which led Mayor Daley to install a 24 hour security team. Hoffman offered to leave the city for $10,000 and the *Chicago Tribune* decried, "Yippies Demand Cash From City." Ultimately, the whole event ended in riots, baton charges and utter chaos. Hoffman went through Chicago with a four letter word painted on his forehead because, he said, it kept his face off the TV screens. Hoffman and Rubin were then arrested and tried as part of the 'Chicago 8', for incitement to riot.

Rubin became a celebrity and was invited to the UK to appear on the *David Frost Show* in 1970. The live show on London Weekend Television erupted into chaos when Rubin lit up a joint wrapped in stars and stripes paper. The spliff lighting was the signal for about 20 UK Yippies, including Mick Farren and *OZ* magazine team Richard Neville and Felix Dennis, to storm the stage, causing mayhem as Frost was sprayed with a water pistol. Police raided the studio but Rubin and his cohorts had already left. The forensic team found cannabis traces in two ends, and a joint containing half a gram of cannabis. Tragically, Rubin sold his socialist dreams and bought into wholesale capitalism, but was run over and killed in LA in 1994.

Meanwhile, Dana Beal and his fellow Yippies started the *YIPster Times* after the Miami Republican Convention protests in 1972. He continued to crusade for marijuana legalization throughout the '70s. Beal then collaborated with Tom Forcade – the infamous cannabis smuggler and founder of *High Times* - and changed the name of the paper to *Overthrow* in 1979. In December the following year, Beal set up 'Rock Against Racism' and initiated an Ibogaine project with Howard Lots. This was an effort to make the addiction interrupter available to drug users everywhere. Always ahead of the game, Beal also advocated medical marijuana for AIDS patients as early as 1986.

Right: The *OZ* team of James Anderson, Richard Neville and Felix Dennis get scalped!

Beal joined the gay activist group ACT UP in 1988, and promoted Ibogaine through ACT UP and the government body, the National Institute on Drug Abuse (NIDA). However, he was fired from the latter when he was revealed to be a medical marijuana activist. After a short prison stint in '93, Beal co-founded an activist group, Cures not Wars, and started the NYC Medical

Marijuana Buyers' Club with Johann Moore in 1995. Beal was part of the Wheelchair Walk for Medical Marijuana from Boston to DC in Fall 1997. In 2003, he got together with fellow activists such as ex-Jefferson Airplane lead singer, Grace Slick, to create a speakers' lecturing bureau to tour America's universities. Patrick Kroupa, 34, a former computer hacker who is also in the speakers' bureau, said students were closer to Yippie ideas than people thought, "The counterculture didn't drop dead," said Kroupa. "It just went online."

And how true that is. Today, if you trawl through the seemingly endless marijuana sites, there are literally hundreds, if not thousands, of pro-cannabis groups across the world. Many are small, self supporting, local action groups who subsist on donations and fund raisers. Many work as coalitions and form unified links with fellow campaigners across the globe. There is a real feeling of camaraderie amongst activists, who are as equally passionate and vehement as the prohibitionists, but without the vast federal reserves to back them up. A constant problem.

Many campaigners focus on single issues, such as the right to use medical marijuana (such as the California based Wo/Men's Alliance for Medical Marijuana – WAMM – whose membership includes writer/philosopher Robert Anton Wilson), or the release of prisoners who have been arrested for cannabis possession. This sea of acronyms (ASA, IMM, UKCIA, AMMA, etc.) can be daunting at first, but there are a few groups that have become internationally recognised as major movers and shakers in getting governmental drug policies changed.

NORML

Possibly the most famous pro-cannabis group in America, if not the world, is the National Organisation for the Reform of Marijuana Laws, better known as NORML.

"Marijuana leads to homosexuality... and therefore to AIDS."

White House Drug Czar, Carlton Turner, 1986.

"Marijuana produces a wide variety of symptoms in the user, including hilarity, swooning, and sexual excitement... it often makes the smoker vicious, with a desire to fight and kill."

Scientific American magazine, 1936.

Founded in 1970 by Keith Stroup, NORML has become one of the most active and vocal thorns in the US government's side. As a non-profit, public interest advocacy group, NORML continues to represent the interests of millions of Americans who smoke marijuana. Stroup is a Washington public interest attorney who has acted as an advocate for artists, family farmers and, of course, for marijuana smokers. He served as the organization's first National Director until 1979. That same year, after nine years of NORML campaigning, marijuana was decriminalized in 11 US States, with at least another 12 States reducing marijuana possession from a criminal offence - carrying jail time - to a civil violation, attracting a small fine. However, in a hangover from Anslinger's vendetta, the drug remained a Schedule I substance under federal law, prohibiting even medical use.

On 18 May 1972, NORML petitioned the Bureau of Narcotics and Dangerous Drugs (now known as the Drug Enforcement Administration or DEA) to downgrade marijuana to Schedule II so that physicians could legally prescribe it. The BNDD refused on the basis of their interpretation of US treaty commitments. Then in 1974, the US Court of Appeals ruled against the government and ordered them to process the petition. The government continued to stall. Three years later, the Court essentially stated that the government had to actually conduct scientific and medical evaluations of marijuana before they could legally ban it as a controlled substance, and in 1980, the Court ordered the government to start the evaluations.

Meanwhile, in 1981, Congress members took action to reschedule the drug legislatively, when the late Stuart McKinney introduced a bill to transfer marijuana to Schedule II. It was surprisingly supported by a coalition of 84 House members, including Newt Gingrich, Bill McCollum, John Porter (Ill), and Frank Wolf. After the bill died in committee, Barney Frank began introducing nearly identical legislation on an annual basis, but so far all of Frank's bills have suffered the same fate.

NORML's 22 year long legal battle to get marijuana downgraded ultimately ended in defeat in 1994. The petition was officially dead. "Each of the doctors testifying on behalf of NORML claimed that his opinion was based on scientific studies, yet with one exception, none could identify, under oath, the scientific studies they relied on," DEA Administrator, Thomas A Constantine remarked in 1995.

Despite this blow, NORML continued to fight to reform state and federal marijuana laws, by voter initiative and through elected legislatures. NORML also provided the media with marijuana related stories, giving an alternative point of view to the anti-cannabis propaganda from the government.

But a surprise overruling in California on 15 August 2000, saw the Appeals Court approve

Right: Despite the huge amount of cannabis seized annually, it barely scrapes the surface.

marijuana as medicine. Then, in November, a study of pot's benefits to AIDS patients even got the DEA's blessing!

The organization's sister group, the NORML Foundation, conducts educational and research activities, and in October 1998 published a high media profile report on US domestic marijuana production. The report estimated the value and number of marijuana plants grown in 1997, and calculated that the DEA, State and local law enforcement agencies seized 32% of domestic marijuana planted that year. According to the report, "Marijuana remains the fourth largest cash crop in America despite law enforcement spending an estimated $10 billion annually to pursue efforts to outlaw the plant." The NORML Foundation also sponsors advertising campaigns to educate the public about marijuana and provides legal assistance and support to victims of prohibition.

NORML now has a huge network of volunteer state and local NORML chapters across America, and internationally, who all organize their own events and campaigns with guidance from the main Board.

In 1992, Keith Stroup received the Richard J Dennis Drugpeace Award for Outstanding Achievement in the Field of Drug Policy Reform from the Drug Policy Foundation. He rejoined the Board of NORML in 1994, and currently serves as the Executive Director.

Left: Actor Woody Harrelson is an ardent campaigner and NORML Board member.

NORML's Board of Directors sets policies and initiatives and is made up of 19 prominent scientists, researchers, businessmen and women, writers, attorneys and producers, including author and commentator Barbara Ehrenreich.

Top celebrities, leading academics and drug policy experts sit on NORML's Advisory Board. Active and high profile Board members include country music star, and long time NORML supporter, Willie Nelson; film director Robert Altman; comedian and political satirist Bill Maher; Lester Grinspoon MD, Harvard Medical School (Emeritus); documentary filmmaker Ron Mann; and actor Woody Harrelson. The last two members collaborated together on the excellent documentary *Grass*, about the history of America's marijuana prohibition, with Mann directing and Harrelson providing the narration.

As NORML's web site points out, "The battle for the hearts and minds of the public is largely fought in the media, and a prestigious advisory board assures NORML greater access to those who shape public opinion."

MAPS

Another high profile, but more recent group aiming to change the hearts and minds of America's moral majority is The Multidisciplinary Association for Psychedelic Studies (MAPS). Not to be confused with MAP (The Media Awareness Project), the most active online campaign that started in 1996, MAPS is yet another non-profit research and educational organization.

Personal Highs:

Pot purveying pensioner

Sixty six year old Grandma Pat, also known as Patricia Tabram, hit the headlines in December when she was busted at her home, a remote bungalow in the village of Humshaugh, in Northumberland, England.

Her crime? Possessing cannabis with intent to supply from her home. When the former chef was introduced to the wonder weed in early 2004, she began sprinkling it into pies, casseroles and cakes, like a modern day Alice B Toklas.

Having switched to Skunk from apparently useless NHS medications, which she says had done her no good at all, Grandma Pat was so startled at the relief it brought to her various aches and pains, she began distributing her discovery among her friends, average age 75, who also reported improvements to their health.

Northumbria Police were tipped off about the savoury smells and activities coming from Tabram's bungalow and twice raided her house in May and June 2004. Tabram protested her innocence, explaining that her consumption had been purely for medicinal purposes. The police though, had other ideas, and said her house, "…bore all the hallmarks of a sophisticated drug dealer."

They found 31 cannabis plants growing in her loft, another one on her hallway table, as well as individual portions of the drug in her fridge and on her bedside cabinet. She met a dealer in Hexham, after her friends said they also wanted some of the Class C drug. Police raided her home a day after she took delivery of the cannabis, "They can put me in prison as long as they like," she said. "I'm not afraid of going to prison. I'll come out and start buying it again. And then they can put me in prison again and I'll come out and start buying it again."

But in April 2005, Judge David Hodson said he would not make a martyr of Patricia Tabram. The grass loving granny was given a six month prison sentence, suspended for two years and a £750 fine.

Outside Newcastle Crown Court, Tabram was unrepentant, "I do intend to continue using cannabis, but I haven't given any to anyone since the day I was arrested. I think it is a better medicine than what you receive from the NHS. But I am no more addicted to cannabis than I am to soap operas. I will continue to go to people's houses and cook for them if people get their own ingredients."

The grass growing granny even stood as the Legalise Cannabis Alliance's parliamentary candidate in the 2005 General Election, against Welsh Secretary Peter Hain, in his Neath constituency. While on the campaign trail she stated, "People think of me as just a pleasant, harmless lady with a cardigan who eats cannabis.

> ## "They can put me in prison as long as they like," she said. "I'm not afraid of going to prison. I'll come out and start buying it again. And then they can put me in prison again and I'll come out and start buying it again."

I am that, I suppose. But I'm also very angry."

She is writing a book about her experiences called *Grandma Eats Cannabis* and even has a web site (www.grandma-eats-cannabis.co.uk) to share her recipes with the world.

Spliffs 3

MAPS helps scientists to obtain approval and funding for research into the healing and spiritual potential of psychedelics and marijuana. Since 1995, MAPS has handed out over $2 million to worthy research and educational projects. A massive amount in reefer research terms.

In the past they've sponsored pioneering analytical research into the effects of marijuana vaporizers, with the first human study of marijuana vaporizers conducted by Dr. Donald Abrams, UC San Francisco. They also funded Dr. Abrams' first human study in 15 years into the therapeutic use of marijuana, along with a $1 million grant from the National Institute on Drug Abuse.

Currently, MAPS is helping Prof. Lyle Craker obtain a license from the Drug Enforcement Administration for a marijuana production facility for research. In February 2005, the DEA's initial rationale for rejecting Prof. Craker's application was that it would be against the public interest for it to approve the license, and in any case, US international treaty obligations prevented the DEA from issuing the license. Still hiding behind the same excuses they used against NORML way back in 1972. Surprisingly, the pre-hearing statement mentioned only the public interest issue, as even the DEA is starting to realize their international treaty claims are weak. Regardless of the DEA's blessings for certain areas of research back in 2000, their policies can be described, at best, as erratic. Recently, MAPS' and MAP's media profiles have been growing to almost equal that of NORML's, as all three groups demand more research into medical marijuana use.

The Drug Policy Alliance
The Drug Policy Foundation was founded in 1987 and soon built up 25,000 supporters. It was the principal membership based organization advocating more sensible and humane drug policies.

Created seven years later, in 1994, The Lindesmith Centre was a leading independent drug policy reform institute in the United States. In September 1998, the organization teamed up with the UK group Release and organized the Options for Control in the 21st Century symposium in London. The one day event saw experts fly in from all over the world to discuss the important issues.

The two organizations merged on 1 July 2000 and became known as The Drug Policy Alliance, with the objective of building a national drug policy reform movement. The guiding principle of the Alliance is harm reduction, an alternative approach to drug policy and treatment that focuses on minimizing the adverse effects of both drug use and drug prohibition. The Alliance also believes educating Americans is the key to legalization.

Right: Medical marijuana users demand legalization.

STOP
Arresting
Patients
FOR MEDICAL
MARIJUANA
PATIENTS
NOT
CRIMINALS

The non-profit (aren't they all?) organization doesn't, "believe that there is an ultimate solution to our drug problems, but we do believe that there are steps that can and should be taken soon to reduce the harms associated with both drug use and our failed policies. These include: making marijuana legally available for medical purposes and ending criminal penalties for marijuana, except those involving distribution of drugs to children."

All three organisations, NORML, MAPS and the Drug Alliance, got together for what was one of the marijuana legalization movement's most ostentatious events in August 2005, the Jamaica based Psytopia.

Rainbow Farm/Victims

But activists have a hard time as well, and there have been many tragic victims. The 'War on Drugs' harms more innocents than it protects, as Jim Montgomery discovered to his cost in 1992. Montgomery, a paraplegic who smoked cannabis to relieve muscle spasm pains, was busted for two ounces of marijuana in Oklahoma, USA. He was arrested and sentenced to life plus 16 years. How the government perceived a wheelchair bound pot smoker to be such threat that he should receive a sentence worse than some murders, remains a mystery. And, tragically, it's not an isolated incident – a court in Texas

Left: Sometimes the 'personal use' argument just won't work with the police.

sentenced another medical marijuana user on 16 January 1997. William J Foster received a 'mere' 93 years' imprisonment. His crime? The cultivation of one plant. With endless cases like these, it's not surprising that campaigners are so passionate. And yet there are even worse cases, and one in particular that shook the cannabis activist movement to the core.

When Tom Crosslin, his boyfriend Rolland Rohm, and Rohm's son Robert, settled at Rainbow Farm, Cass County, Michigan in 1993 it was with high hopes in every sense. Tired of seeing friends, relatives and others jailed because of marijuana use, and having seen too many families destroyed, just for the use of a god given herb, Tom Crosslin finally announced, "We're going to throw hemp festivals here!"

Crosslin did his research and allowed visitors to smoke on his land. Smoking is a misdemeanour in Michigan, but technically, the cops can't enter private property to issue a ticket for a misdemeanour. Gathering to smoke pot in the house, Crosslin knew, would constitute a felony, 'Maintaining a drug house', but no law existed for an open field. It was a thin green line, which protected all of them for a while.

In 1996, the first two annual Rainbow Farm events, HempAid held on Memorial Day, and Roach Roast on Labour Day, were part Woodstock, part picnic. They were family oriented affairs, with soft drink stands, hemp clothing vendors and representatives from NORML. Onstage speakers railed against government oppression. Guests included *High Times* editor Steve Hager, and MC5 manager John Sinclair, who was sentenced to 10 years in prison for possessing two joints in 1969.

From 1996 to 2001, Rainbow Farm became the centre of pot activism in Michigan. The events cost more than $100,000 each to put on, and Crosslin needed to sell 2,500 tickets just to break even. "We were pretty much operating to keep operating," said event promoter Derrik DeCraene. Crosslin felt that the shows would eventually become viable, but his determination to build Rainbow Farm into a private utopia was getting in the way of profitability. "It was a beautiful thing. If we were a humanitarian project, we would have gotten awards. But instead we were made out to be villains and pot smokers," DeCraene remembered.

Crosslin was determined that there should be no hard drugs allowed, and felt that if a marijuana high isn't good enough anymore, get better marijuana. The whole point of the gatherings was to show the world that you can use marijuana and be responsible.

At the start of 1999, Crosslin's organizers improved the festivals' profiles, buying lighted signboards along Highway M-60. But the higher profile brought unwanted attention. Bob File believed the signs brought trouble, "If Tom had been more discreet," recalled the neighbour, "there wouldn't have been much they could do. But once he pissed those guys off, there was no turning back." Cass County prosecutor Scott

Teter was one of those Crosslin had pissed off. "Crosslin believed in the legalization of marijuana," Teter said. "I don't have any problem with that – in fact, our system encourages it. But at some point, his gatherings became 'Come to this property and use, distribute and deal any narcotic you choose'."

Teter began harassing Rainbow Farm in December 1996. On Memorial Day, the sheriff and the State police set up a checkpoint on the only road to the farm. All weekend, cars were stopped and ticketed. Teter said he didn't want to start a war, "We made a decision several years ago that for misdemeanour use of marijuana, I was not going marshal 500 troops and go in and provoke a violent confrontation."

But word was getting out that you'd be harassed – or worse – if you went to Rainbow Farm. Ticket sales dropped. In 1998 Teter sent an undercover narc into the festivals but couldn't find enough evidence to prosecute the organizers. He sent a letter, "putting Crosslin on notice" and claiming that he knew about, "hard drugs" there. When fliers went up announcing HempAid '99, Teter sent another letter, threatening to seize Crosslin's property if hard drugs were found.

"That fucking son of a bitch, who does he think he is?" ranted Crosslin, and shot back his reply. "I have discussed this with my family, and

Right: In 1971, over 15,000 people attended a rally in Ann Arbor to free John Sinclair (pictured right) from jail.

we are all prepared to die on this land before we allow it to be stolen from us. How should we be prepared to die? Are you planning to burn us out like they did in Waco, or will you have snipers shoot us through our windows like the Weavers at Ruby Ridge?"

"Well, that sort of set the tone that we weren't going to be able to talk this thing out," Teter said. "Crosslin was saying, 'I'm going to do what I'm going to do, and I don't think that you're going to do anything about it', but I took an oath to do something about it." What had been a political chess match turned into a blood feud.

"Tom wasn't eloquent, but he was articulate on his points," recalled friend, Don France. "In essence, it was, 'Leave private citizens alone. If they want to smoke a little pot, they can smoke a little pot. If they want to grow it and make a product out of it, well and good too.'"

Despite Teter's attempts to shut down Rainbow Farm, HempAid '99 went ahead as planned and turned out to be the best ever. Tommy Chong and his sons played to 2,800 people who'd paid $65 each. The fact that Crosslin was able to pull it off in the face of Teter's obstacles thrilled his employees and national pot activists.

Undaunted, Teter had sent in undercover narcs during both festivals in 1999 and secretly videoed naked hippies and people of all kinds

Left: Pot protests on the streets of Washington DC were more vocal in the Sixties. Rise up!

getting stoned, presenting an unflattering picture of Rainbow Farm to the courts. 2000 was financially hard for Crosslin and his crew, so they went on an all out push to make money and added the *High Times* World Hemp Entertainment Expo and a concert by Merle Haggard to their schedule. But the events lost $45,000 because of poor advertising and the Farm's growing narc reputation.

The following year, Crosslin and Rohm decided to build a hydroponic room for growing pot in the farmhouse's basement. "We were the biggest pot activists in the state of Michigan, for crying out loud," said DeCraene: "But they were so high profile they couldn't get any pot. And this was their solution."

On 9 May 2001, DeCraene woke up with Michigan State troopers in ski masks pointing guns at his head. "The cops were so scared, their gun barrels were shaking. I'm thinking... Oh my god! These guys are going to shoot me and just say they thought I was trying to draw a weapon."

The heavily armed squad had come to support the IRS on a tax warrant. But the troopers found the grow room and confiscated 301 starter plants, along with a loaded 9mm pistol and two loaded shotguns. Crosslin and Rohm were busted for manufacturing marijuana (a 15 year maximum sentence), firearms violations and for maintaining a drug house (each carrying two year sentences). The bust was big news. Teter got an injunction banning all future festivals. By the time Crosslin and Rohm were out on bail, Teter had already filed for the forfeiture of Rainbow Farm.

Then Teter made it personal by taking Rohm's son, Robert, and putting him in foster care. Crosslin felt he'd failed. His festivals were a bust. His employees had been forced to leave. He had no money. His corner of the world had been invaded; his lifestyle and his vision crushed. Things went from bad to worse when Crosslin and Rohm burnt their farm buildings down and sat and waited, armed, for the police.

Buggy Brown, a regular at Rainbow Farm, was milking cows when he saw smoke pouring into the sky. He rushed to the farm and found Rohm dressed in camouflage, carrying a Ruger Mini-14 .223 ranch rifle. Brown sized things up and said, "Smoke one last bowl?" They fired one up in Brown's pipe as the buildings burned to a crisp and then Rohm said, "It's time. You need to leave." Brown, upset, called Sheriff Joe Underwood, who sealed off the only way in or out. Later, a TV news helicopter and a Michigan State police plane were shot at. The FBI arrived at Rainbow Farm and the siege began.

By nightfall, State police snipers had crawled into positions in the woods. Inside the house, Crosslin and Rohm were drinking beer. They had no electricity, no phone, and no water. On Saturday morning, the FBI took over communications, with Brown as an intermediary, who began by saying, "I want to tell you right now, I'm a pot smoker." When Teter showed up at the command post, Brown threatened to quit unless he left. The FBI forced Teter away.

By dawn on Labour Day 2001, 120 law enforcement officers were on the scene. That morning, Brandon Peoples, an 18 year old neighbour, managed to slip past the cops, determined to convince Crosslin to turn himself in. Crosslin was pissed off to see him but needed help to scrounge some food from a neighbour's abandoned cabin. Crosslin carried his gun and a two way radio and stepped outside. On the way back from a successful forage, Peoples heard shots and shouting. FBI snipers popped up and shot Crosslin above the right eye and blew out the back of his skull, killing him instantly. His brain landed two feet away from his shattered head. Skull fragments raked the face of Peoples, who went down on his hands and knees screaming, "I'm hit!" The agents moved in quickly and placed him under arrest. Crosslin never fired his gun. Rohm waited in the house alone.

Rohm agreed to surrender at seven o'clock the following morning, if he saw his son. The FBI agreed. But just after 6am, an upper room in the house caught fire, and Rohm emerged, carrying his gun. According to the police, they stormed up and told Rohm to drop the gun. He seemed frightened and confused. Suddenly he turned back into the house. He re-emerged on the run and took cover under a small pine tree 10 yards

Right: MPP activists demonstrate outside the US Supreme Court.

from the house, where was shot by a sniper. One bullet went through the butt of his rifle and his chest. Like Crosslin, he never fired a shot.

"This was a Waco-like event," said Rick Martinez, Michigan editor for the *South Bend Tribune*. The official version of events – that Crosslin and Rohm both raised their rifles – was soon disputed. The story was quickly overshadowed by the events of 9/11, and so the brief and tragic battle in the ongoing war on drugs was buried.

The UK experience

While there is a common enemy in the governments of the world and their outdated laws, not all the lobby and action groups get on with each other all the time. In 2003, there was a storm in a teacup between Dana Beal and NORML, over his quickly growing international May Day demonstrations.

"The idea that there is some kind of anti-NORML bias in the Million Marijuana March Coalition is patently ridiculous," announced Beal. "Look at who's putting on the marches. It's all local NORML chapters! And national NORML propaganda is being distributed at them. If someone at the National Office or on the NORML Board really has such a big problem with public rallies and marches, all you can say is that I'm helping them out in spite of themselves."

Left: The lions of Trafalgar Square, London enjoy a toke at a 1998 demo.

Dismissing the rumours and innuendo, the perennial crusader Beal went on, "Far better to go out and recruit a hundred new cities than to infight." And that's exactly what he did when he visited London.

When Beal went to the UK's capital in 1999 to suggest the first weekend in May as a date for a co-ordinated set of worldwide cannabis marches, an assembled coalition of UK cannabis campaigners leapt at the idea. Beal initiated the Million Marijuana March and it was to become the most vocal and visible public rage against the prohibition machine. By 2003, over 230 cities had joined Beal's vision of a global event demanding the legalization of cannabis. Now, countries as diverse as New Zealand, Argentina and Hungary, and cities from Oslo and Paris to Warsaw and Nashville all take part with their own demonstrations, festivals and events. May Day has undoubtedly become Jay Day!

The first London march and festival took place on May Day 1999 with 10,000 people marching through south London, arriving at the festival site on Clapham Common. The event harked back to the Hyde Park events in '67. Then, the local council tried to prosecute the festival when people were spotted dancing (which was prohibited!). But the courts overruled the council.

The following year, 2000, the event was granted an entertainment license, and 30,000 people revelled, rolled and reeled in the spring sunshine. Organizers negotiated with the Metropolitan Police not to carry out arrests for

"**Marijuana is self punishing. It makes you acutely sensitive and, in this world, what worse punishment could there be?**"

PJ O'Rourke, author.

"I've never had a
problem with drugs.
I've had problems
with the police."

Keith Richards, Rolling Stones.

possession, and so cannabis was essentially decriminalised for the day in Lambeth.

2001's event was a washout, having been postponed until June due to the rain. It still rained on the day, but despite the soggy joints, thousands still turned up and carried on dancing regardless. Once again, the council tried to prosecute the festival for breach of license, claiming a drink had been distributed 20 minutes after the drinks license had finished, and that *85 seconds* of a tune had been played after the entertainment license had expired. Both attempts were thrown out with the judge wondering why this prosecution had been brought to her court, commenting that the festival organizers, "ran a tight ship."

The one day festival was refused recognition as a non-profit community event, and was charged as a fully commercial organization. Excessive charges have been levied on the festival over the years in order to financially cripple it, but to no avail. The 'free' festival costs over £55,000 to mount, and relies on huge amounts of voluntary labour to produce.

In 1988, in the UK alone, 23,229 people were arrested for cannabis offences, the majority of which were for unlawful possession under the Misuse of Drugs Act 1971. Five years later, in 1993, the figure had more than trebled to 72,000. But by 2000, the number of arrests had dropped to 70,306. When you consider that in 1990, only 30 tonnes of cannabis were seized – yet by 2000, 74 tonnes were captured – it appears that while there's more marijuana around, the British police are less inclined to prosecute. And that's probably down to the large burden on both police time and money.

In 1999, a straightforward caution took an average of three hours of police time. A typical arrest took five hours to process and cost £10,000 to bring to court, yet the average fine was just £46. It eventually reached the point where it wasn't worth the police effort to bust people for pot any more.

British prohibition began to soften when Commander Brian Paddick of Lambeth Police stated that local police would focus their energies on crack and smack, and desist arrests for personal cannabis possession. The 'Lambeth experiment' became a pilot scheme and took off.

A local straw poll showed 83% support for the police's new policy. Brixton, for a brief time, became a 'Little Amsterdam'. Suddenly, the newspapers were full of people in favour of legalization and the then Home Secretary, David Blunkett, announced the Lambeth pilot would be applied nationwide. It ultimately led to Blunkett announcing the reclassification of cannabis in Parliament on 10 July 2002. 18 months later, in January 2004, cannabis was downgraded from a class B to a class C drug; something that NORML has been trying to achieve in the States for over 30 years.

Right: Howard Marks and Rosie Boycott at 1997's pro-cannabis march.

Canada

Like Mexico, Canada has been a constant thorn in America's side in the war against wacky baccy. With its more liberal laws and generally progressive approach, Canada has long been hailed by activists as an example of how to move forward. This goes as far back as the 1970-'73 Le Dain Report, which recommended that serious consideration be given to the legalization of personal possession of marijuana, "It finds that cannabis use increases self confidence, feelings of creativity and sensual awareness, facilitates concentration and self acceptance, reduces tension, hostility and aggression and may produce psychological but not physical dependence. The report recommends that possession laws be repealed."

In October 2000, it was rumoured that the Canadian government would legalize medical marijuana, and two months later it allowed the first legally licensed grow operation. But medical marijuana users still existed in a legal limbo.

That same year saw Marc-Boris St-Maurice, the leader of the Marijuana Party, arrested for selling marijuana at Montreal's Compassion Club, where it is sold to those with a doctor's note.

St-Maurice believed the government must widen its exemption system to allow any patient with a doctor's prescription to obtain the drug, "The government has reacted in a very short

Left: Activist communities like Christiania, Copenhagen, protect the herb.

sighted way. They haven't addressed the issue of doctors and prescriptions," the campaigner said. "They haven't tied up all the loose ends. They're far from being done with us." However, on 30 July 2001, the Narcotic Control Regulations were amended and the Marihuana Medical Access Regulations came into force. This created a compassionate framework for sufferers of cancer, AIDS and similar conditions, or the terminally ill, to use marijuana where the medical benefit outweighed the risk of use. The Office of Cannabis Medical Access allowed patients to apply for a photo ID card which gives them permission to possess, buy or grow marijuana.

Technically, marijuana is still an illegal drug in Canada, but for how long remains the only question. Particularly after a judge announced, in 2002, that medical cannabis was not illegal. But there are constant external pressures from America and the UN Narcotics Control Board, who continually question Canada's marijuana policies.

Despite the good work that continues in Canada and around the world, there is still much to do. There's such a vast amount of dissent, protest and pro-cannabis lobbying, that it's impossible to record it all in one book. But despite the size of the anti-prohibition struggle, it still receives little, if any, real mainstream media coverage. Most newspapers still persist with the tired 'Reefer Madness' propaganda, claiming that cannabis turns ordinary people into killers. Funny that; it's almost enough to make you think there's a conspiracy suppressing legalization…

Chapter 3

Heavenly Hemp

There's no escaping it, hemp is everywhere, and probably already in the homes of even its staunchest opponents. It could be hiding in the nip and tuck of their re-sealable sandwich bags – yup, hemp seed oil derivatives are used by many manufacturers to ensure your bags open and close smoothly time and time again. Or perhaps there is cannabis sativa hiding in those high-tech speakers they just bought. The Alcons Audio speaker, the VR12, features the unique 'Hemp Horn' which is celebrated in the industry for its stiffness, combined with a much higher internal damping than the normal glass fibre horns. A superior product due to the pure blast of the bast.

Heavenly Hemp

The prolific, and occasionally surreptitious, use of hemp comes as no surprise to anyone who's taken a close look at its long and illustrious industrial career, but following almost 70 years of prohibition, hemp is having to fight its way back to its rightful place in the global market.

Hemp was widely used until the 1930s, when it became marginalized by the rise of the pharmaceutical and petrochemical giants who now dominate the world markets. Synthetic fabrics, plastics, paper, fertilizers, pesticides, cotton and the tobacco industry took over, almost wiping out thousands of years of hemp production and use across the globe. But in these times of increasing environmental concern, and when many in the West are looking for sustainable products to support a sustainable world, hemp looks set to make a comeback.

Hemping the Environment

In their visionary books, Chris Conrad (*Hemp Lifeline to the Future*) and Jack Herer (*The Emperor Wears no Clothes* – see page 128) lay out a persuasive argument for hemp as the great healer of our planet. Hemp is an incredibly versatile and tough plant – you can grow it organically virtually anywhere, at any altitude and in many climates. Using hemp instead of fossil fuels, trees and other limited resources could have huge environmental benefits. It can fuel a whole variety of sustainable industries and improve the overall health of our planet by reducing industrial and agricultural emissions, not to mention its 50,000 commercial uses. Uniquely diverse, hemp is already used to make 5,000 textile products and 25,000 cellulose products

Right: Cannabis grows easily everywhere, including this crop in the Lebanon.

Left: Hemp is the most versatile plant on the planet, yet it remains illegal. Why?

from the woody stem alone, the part of the plant described by Chris Conrad as, "The building block of modern industry."

Different strains of hemp have been developed, depending on which part of the plant is to be harvested – the stalk, seeds or the herbal resins from the flowers and leaves. The stalk can be made into fabric, paper, paints, building materials, animal bedding and fuel; the seeds produce cooking oils, fuel, lubricants, lotions and nutritious human and animal food; the foliage can be turned into potent medicines for mind, body and spirit, and medicine for our planet too – the beautiful leaves absorb our excessive carbon dioxide output and transmute it back to clean, fresh air.

All these factors are increasingly important in our world of dwindling finite resources, deforestation, ozone depletion and rocketing oil prices. "Economic strength will increasingly depend on sound environmental policy. If we do not find the vision and leadership to defeat the unprecedented new threats of global climate change, ozone depletion, habitat destruction and desertification, then those threats may well defeat us." – President Bill Clinton in the *LA Times*, 1992. Not if hemp has its way.

Right: Vietnamese women selling their woven, indigo dyed, hemp hats in Sapa.

Use of hemp goes back to prehistoric times. Fragments of cord and fabric have been found in excavations across the globe, testimony to both the wide use of the plant and the extreme durability of the fibre. Pottery fragments embedded with hemp cord, dating from about 8,000 BC, have been found in Taiwan and China (4,000 BC), along with elongated, rod shaped tools used for teasing cannabis fibres from their stems. From around the same time, we have humanity's oldest relic – a small piece of hemp fabric found in an area of what is now Turkey.

Hemp agriculture and industry were also part of the ancient civilizations of the Egyptians, Babylonians, Persians, Hebrews, Chaldeans, Scythians, Romans and Japanese, and by the time we reach the end of the First century AD, it has found its way to Europe as well. Up until the time of the Black Death in England, flax was virtually unknown, while hemp was widespread. It was a crucial product for seafaring and war mongering nations for use in sails and ropes; King Philip of Spain issued a writ in 1564 ordering 'canamo' to be grown throughout his kingdom to supply his fleet and army. Hemp cultivation travelled to America with the first settlers, and in 1619, America's first marijuana law was enacted as Jamestown Colony, Virginia ordered all farmers to, "make tyral of" (i.e. grow) Indian hemp seed. This was followed by similar laws across the States into the mid-1700s, the primary use being for fibre. In his diary of 1794, US President George Washington told his people

to, "Make the most you can of the Indian hemp seed and sow it everywhere." In the 16th century, French philosopher Rabelais could not envisage life without hemp products, "Without it [hemp] how could water be drawn from the well? What would scribes, copyists, secretaries and writers do without it? Would not official documents and rent rolls disappear? Would not the noble art of printing disappear?"

Although hemp was the first plant cultivated by man, with fibre and textile industries sprouting 10,000 years ago simultaneously in China and Eurasia, it is now only grown and manufactured in a few areas due to international paranoia over a different use of cannabis. Although industrial hemp has very low levels of the intoxicant THC, it has taken time for the modern hemp industry to seal this message in the minds of government leaders. Such antics as that of a young enthusiast stealing a cartload of weed from a German farm in the heyday of the 1970s, have only stirred the cauldron. Germany tried to ban hemp growing after this, only to come across the EEC's rules, which protect the industry as part of an old tradition with a rightful place in the modern business world.

When Britain joined the European Community in 1993, the Home Office was obliged to grant hemp farmers commercial farming permits in line with the rest of Europe, and by the early 1990s it had become a subsidized industry. Hemp growing is still illegal across the US since the 1937 ban on all types of cannabis sativa.

Above: The world's greatest cash crop. British hemp grown under a government licence.

Theoretically, the American government will grant licenses to grow industrial hemp, but the Drugs Enforcement Agency would require the farmer to put up a high, razor wire fence and lighting, and mount guard and dog patrols.

Hemp paper is a famously strong, versatile, ecologically sound product which is resistant to water, and which will last for thousands of years. China developed the first hemp paper using a, "mixture of flax and hemp", and the first hemp book, printed in 770 AD, was a Chinese book or prayers called the Dharani. Chinese hemp is still leading the way. Today, as much as 70% of China's paper is made with

83

bast fibres such as hemp, crop residues and recycled cotton instead of pulp.

Until the 1850s, the West used hemp for as much as 75-90% of its paper for books, maps, bibles, banknotes and newspapers. After the 1850s, tree pulping and drastic deforestation began. Now, 93% of the world's paper is from timber (only 29% being recycled) with 226 million trees felled in 1988, a figure which will have tripled in line with current growth by 2020. Chris Conrad estimates that each ton of paper made from hemp will save 12 trees. Once you have recycled this tough product seven times, your original ton has saved 84 trees.

Hemp paper is made from the stalk, with the longest fibres being used for the strongest card and paper, and the shortest for the finest – a favourite for the Bible due to its thinness and its strength. Hemp for paper is a very economic crop, producing more than four times the amount of pulp per hectare as 'old growth' timber and a new crop each year, and it's tough too. There is a new meaning to the pound being strong against the dollar – hemp is still used in the UK's currency, which lasts three times longer than the hemp free US dollar. Virtually all stocks and bonds are printed on hemp paper and, ironically, so were the first two drafts of the American Declaration of Independence.

Left: *Cannabis ruderalis* is tall and skinny, unlike its THC-rich stubby cousins, *sativa* and *indica*.

Hemp paper is made by breaking down the woody hurds in the plant stem with a soda process. Unlike timber pulp, it does not need powerful sulphur based chemicals to break it down, and so hemp paper can even reduce the chemical pollution of our rivers by 60%-80%. The main drawback with hemp paper is that slightly more string remains after pulping hemp than trees, leaving a slightly rougher finish, but as money is invested in the industry to refine the technologies, such details should be ironed out. Financial cost is another factor, but once economies of scale are introduced, this again should be minimized, with the added value of vastly reduced environmental costs compared to modern paper making. The answer to so many of our environmental concerns appears to be written in hemp.

Biomass – A hemp fuelled future

Biomass, basically, refers to a shit load of something – in this case hemp – grown in one place for use in industry. Western industries are looking to plants to provide fuel for power stations and heavy industry, with the best sources being woody and high in lignocellulose. Hemp is just such a plant. A study at the University of Hawaii found that biomass could meet up to 90% of that State's energy requirements, and worldwide it looks like a viable way of complementing other alternative energy sources – solar, wind and hydroelectricity – but with less restrictions on where it can be harnessed. Hemp will grow virtually anywhere, and the same soil can be used in cultivation for many years without any drop in yield. Once hemp is grown widely again, it will provide more and more of the Earth's biomass for industry.

Not only does hemp appear to be a viable fuel option, it looks like it will be financially cheaper too. A report in the *LA Times* in 1992 stated, "Marijuana burns at extremely high temperatures and gives off considerable heat energy. Burning marijuana would be cheaper than coal and produce about as much energy." Another big plus is that hemp burns very cleanly compared to fossil fuels.

Biomass has previously been used as fuel in Asia, and briefly in America during their 'Hemp For Victory' campaign during the Second World War, and the UK's first power station to run on biomass is Drax Power Ltd in North Yorkshire. Currently using short rotation willow coppice, hemp could be Drax's fuel of the future – along with many other power stations – if the UK government is to reach its target of 20% of electricity coming from renewable energy sources by 2020.

The growth of the hemp biomass industry could, "revolutionise British Farming" according to the BBC's Environment Correspondent, Yvette Austin, and farmers are keen to cash in. The National Farmers Union in the UK's South West is encouraging farmers in the area to diversify by growing cannabis and adding to the 3,000 hectares of industrial hemp already

growing in Britain under license from the Home Office. Growing hemp for biomass is a subsidized industry, and in 2004 the Arable Area Payments Scheme paid farmers £246.13 per hectare to grow hemp, and £64.54 per tonne of the plant toward fibre processing costs. Licenses avoid confusion with hemp's psychotropic sister, cannabis sativa, but the National Non-Food Crops Centre admits that the physical similarity of the plants create, "policing problems." However, "Work is in progress to produce cultivators with zero THC, and to develop visual or simple field diagnosis tests for these types." So there wouldn't be much point in picking these buds and rolling a spliff. The only high you're going to get is from the farmer greeting you.

Hemp housing and the smart little pig

Everyone mocked the little pig who built his house of straw, but from a 21st century perspective it looks like he had the last laugh. Hemp housing is happening, and the main part of the plant to be used is the woody stalk. This is chipped and then blended with hydraulic lime and water to make a plaster like substance, which is pressed between a wooden framework like cement. The result is an incredibly strong organic material, which will last for generations. The material allows the house to 'breathe' and eventually decomposes harmlessly back into the earth. The world's first biodegradable house!

"Most modern construction methods,

especially cement, are very high carbon monoxide producers, but hemp, timber and lime reduce carbon monoxide levels in the air," reported Helen Bruce in *The Irish Times* on Ireland's first hemp house. "A model of eco-construction," the house has been made to look as far as possible like a conventional home. It is however, a much more economical home to heat, saving 10-20% on fuel bills due to its excellent insulation properties.

Another exciting hemp housing project is currently being overseen by the UK's Suffolk Housing Department. Four identical houses are being built – two out of conventional brick and wood, and two out of hemp and lime. "The 'Hemp Homes' project is an innovative and exciting experiment which tries to identify the true environmental and commercial advantages of building homes using this particularly ecological and highly sustainable building material," said a spokesperson for the Department for the Environment, Food and Rural Affairs in December 2004.

While hemp homes are having their initial test runs, hemp building materials are already on the market. There are a whole range of building products from various weights of compressed agricultural fibreboard, insulation panels and, coming soon, hemp breeze blocks. Fibreboard is made by grinding or chopping hemp stalks, then

Left: A Tasmanian hemp farmer checks his crop for fibre growth.

"If alcohol is a tiger, cannabis is merely a mouse."

Rosie Boycott, Independent on Sunday,
28 September 1997.

"Much virtue in herbs, little in men."

Benjamin Franklin, US politician/inventor.

bonding it together with natural resins or glues and clamping it into moulds under high pressure. The resultant panels are strong enough to be load bearing, have an excellent resistance to earthquakes, provide good insulation and sound proofing, are immune to termite infestations, mould and decay, and are naturally fire resistant.

Over 300 houses have been built in France using these materials, at the same costs as a standard building, despite the market still being in its infancy. There is great faith amongst builders and industrialists in these new hemp products, and the UK's biggest processor of hemp fibre, Hemcore, describes hemp as, "the greenest natural fibre available today." Hemcore specializes in the expanding area of hemp insulation fibre. "More and more homeowners are looking for natural materials to insulate their properties and are starting to value and appreciate this new use of hemp."

Hemcore has UK farmers growing around 300 hectares of industrial hemp, which is processed at their Essex factory where the hemp plant is separated out into bast fibre and core. The inner core is chipped and sold as top quality horse bedding, and the inner fibre is either sold to European paper, car and insulation businesses, or made into hemp wool for insulation. Once the fibres are separated from the stalk, a fire retardant treatment is applied and some polyester is added. The mixture is then heated in an oven until the polyester fuses and links the hemp fibres. The result is a roll of 'hemp wool' – an insulation material with all the properties of conventional glass wool, and the added benefits of regulating humidity in the home and being completely biodegradable. The drawback is that hemp wool is still relatively expensive, and so eco-building initiatives are calling for government assistance for those who opt for this ecological alternative, similar to those in place for solar energy.

Once your house of hemp stalks is built, it can be painted and varnished using hemp oil products. With your hemp curtains blowing in the breeze coming off the surrounding hemp fields, and a tasty hemp loaf in the oven, you quickly grease the squeaking hinge on your kitchen door with a drop of hemp oil before sitting down for a pre-dinner spliff, smiling at the bygone days when the big bad wolf used to knock on your door.

Hemp plastics back on the road

There seems to be nothing that hemp can't do, especially as cellulose in the stalks makes a very moldable, durable and ecologically sound plastic. It's hard to imagine a world without plastics; they're everywhere. Most come from petrochemicals and are virtually indestructible – hence the permanent rubbish mountains which scar every city on the planet. Far more ecologically viable plastics used to be made from plant based cellulose. Indeed, the first plastics were made from cotton cellulose and the first synthetic fabric nylon was made from wood derived rayon. Time again to turn back the clock, but with a modern twist.

Above: Indoor hemp growing isn't recommended, but is a necessity in the USA.

Hemp, wheat straw and sisal were the main ingredients in Henry Ford's famous 1941 prototype bio-plastic car. Great things were expected from this marijuana mobile. It was about a third of the weight of a normal steel car, could withstand ten times more impact without denting and, designed to run on plant power, was more fuel efficient. Unfortunately, Prohibition stalled the vehicle just as it was

91

picking up speed, and only now are innovative industrialists jump starting the bandwagon and beginning to work again with hemp plastics.

Ben Dronkers' HempFlax company produces pressed hemp fibre for panels and dashboards, and French company Techni-Lin supplied flax based door panels for the Opal Corsa, Citroen C5 and the rear shelf for the Renault Twingo. Hemp insulating fibre is used within these panels and is favoured over glass fibre in the auto trade as it is both lighter and cheaper. "In Europe there is a wealth of interest in composites made from natural fibres," reported Francois Asselin, the manager at Techni-Lin. It's only a matter of time until hemp plastic takes the world by storm. BMW is currently experimenting with hemp materials in their cars in an attempt to make them more readily recycled and it won't be long before Henry Ford's dream of cheap hemp cars and hemp plastics is back on the road.

Methanol – hemp on the move

Once your marijuana mobile is moving, you'll need to stop to fill it up. Yet again, hemp has the answer. Instead of petrol – another dwindling finite resource which is highly damaging to the atmosphere at all stages of production and which has fuelled more than one modern day war – there's methanol, the pot fuel produced from dried fragments of the hemp stalk.

Early attempts to produce and market hemp based fuels for cars and industry were effectively halted by Prohibition back in 1937. Today the know how and the technology already exists. It simply needs to be broadened and fine tuned and more hemp grown, for pot petrol to become a world fuel staple.

In the mid 20th century, Henry Ford's biomass pyrolysis plant in Michigan was designed to run a fleet of bio-cars, including his famous Model T. Pyrolysis was the process of heating organic matter in a vacuum, and the techniques can be adapted to produce a range of fuels including charcoal, pyrolytic oil, methane gas or methanol.

But is it actually possible to grow enough biomass fuel to run the New Green World? Chris Conrad believes it is. A single acre of hemp produces around 1,000 gallons of methane annually, so only about 6% of US farmland would need to grow biomass in order to supply the entire nation's current demands for oil and gas – without pumping carbon dioxide into the atmosphere.

Ethanol and methanol fuels produced from biomass have a higher octane rating than petrol, and produce less carbon monoxide, hydrocarbons and nitrogen oxide emissions due to their lower burning temperatures. Not only are we looking at a sustainable source of fuel for vehicles and manufacturing industries, we are looking at one which can be grown organically and which pours oxygen back into the atmosphere as it grows. And yet cannabis remains illegal!

Right: Kelly Wiglesworth, of TV's Survivor, poses in a hip hemp dress by Minawear.

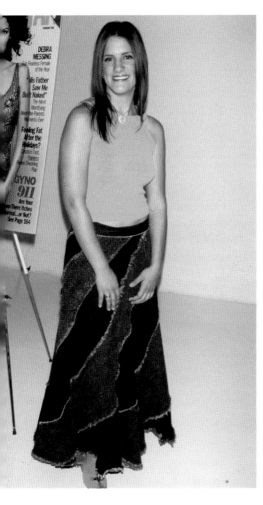

Hemp – the fabric of fashion

Hemp fabric has a glorious and ancient history. Textiles were the first known use of hemp and are sacred to the Japanese Shintos as a symbol of purity. Recently, hemp fabric has become more associated with all things green and good.

Well processed - from the long bast fibres in the stem – and expertly made, hemp produces a material as fine as linen, as Herodotus, the Greek 'Father of History', observed in 450 BC when he came across some hemp fabric in Thrace, "There is in that country kannabis growing, both wild and cultivated. Fuller and taller than flax, the Thracians use it to make garments very like linen. Unless one were a Master of Hemp, one could not tell which it was. Those who have never seen hemp would think it was flax."

Until Prohibition, hemp was a prized fabric, as noted by Brent Moore in his 1905 book, *The Hemp Industry in Kentucky*. Moore wrote, "Such is the competition to purchase hemp that it always brings the last cent that the manufacturer can afford to pay." Modern hemp supplies continue to be stretched to the limit, with the result that the fibre is often over lengthened, meaning that much modern hemp fabric has a tendency to shrink. Good designers pre-shrink their lines and the inventive ones include hemp rayon in their repertoire. The current scarcity of hemp inspires many to cotton or linen mixes, and pure hemp, "is one of the world's rarest and most expensive fabrics," according to Chris Conrad.

Pro-pot politics

Politics and marijuana have always been entwined but no more so than in the UK, where campaigning has been taken to new heights with pro-cannabis candidates running for parliament.

When the General Election was called in 1997, The Campaign to Legalise Cannabis Association (CLCIA) announced their parliamentary candidates. The Legalise Cannabis Party, sponsored by the CLCIA, nominated Howard Marks as their candidate and a plaque was placed on a park bench in Chapelfield Gardens in Norwich, to commemorate Marks' stand.

Norwich City Council then banned the CLCIA from running a market stall because cannabis seeds had been given out. The seeds were fishing bait. After a letter campaign, the council agreed that the CLCIA could have the stall, provided they agree not to give out, "anything, which can be used to grow or take an illegal substance." Norwich soon became the focal point for pro-pot politics.

1997 was THE year of political activism. Advocates received a major boost from an unlikely media source on 28 September when the UK newspaper *The Independent on Sunday*, launched its campaign to decriminalize cannabis. Over 100 celebrities, doctors and academics backed the whole, brave movement. The launch was celebrated with a picnic in Chapelfield Gardens to commemorate the prohibition laws. Over 100 people openly smoked dope in front of the TV cameras.

Two months later on 11 December, *The Independent on Sunday* held its 'Should cannabis be decriminalised?' conference in Westminster, London. All MPs and 'Drugs Czar', Keith Hellawell, were invited to take part, but Hellawell declined and only five MPs turned up.

The event was chaired by TV newsreader Jon Snow, and Body Shop creator and former owner Anita Roddick spoke on the panel. The conference was an overwhelming success and was ultimately, and unsurprisingly, in favour of legalization.

In the General Election, Howard Marks received an average of 1.3% of the vote in the four constituencies in which he stood.

The following year (1998) on 28 March, *The Independent on Sunday* organized the Decriminalise Cannabis March with the CLCIA and others. Over 15,000 people marched from Hyde Park to Trafalgar Square to listen to speakers like Marks, *Independent* editor Rosie Boycott, Paul Flynn MP and Caroline Coon. Unfortunately, soon after the event the *Independent* gave up its pro-cannabis campaign.

In March 1999, The Legalise Cannabis Alliance became an official political party in the UK. In that year's by-elections, the pro-cannabis lobby stood in Norwich (again!), and The Legalise Cannabis Alliance's candidate, Colin Paisley, gained 141 votes in the Kensington and Chelsea by-election – coming eighth out of 18 candidates.

The Legalise Cannabis Alliance fielded five candidates in 2000's Norwich local elections (Sarah Homes, Michael Pryce, Hugh Robertson, Trevor Smith, Christina Smith) and one in Peterborough (Marcus Davies).

In 1998, Danny Tungate polled 7.6% of the vote as a Legalise Cannabis Candidate in the UK

Above: Caroline Coon, co founder of Release, a group offering legal aid to those busted for drugs.

local elections in the Catton Grove ward, Norwich.

The LCA has continued 'growing' until the 2005 General Election, when they had no fewer than 18 candidates in 21 constituencies, one of them being the infamous Grandma Pat, a 61 year old lady who was arrested for cooking with cannabis. (*see feature on page 56*)

Politics and pot seem to be stuck with each other until legalization, and probably beyond.

Above: Ex-President George Washington enjoyed hemp's versatility.

Above: Sowing the seeds of love. Hemp helps enrich the soil where it's planted.

Hemp is the ultimate eco-textile; it's durable, keeps you warm, allows the body to breathe and yes, hemp is cool, in every sense.

Current hemp fashions are steering away from hippy kaftans and flowing robes in favour of the slick and hip. The Hemp Trading Company – THTC – has a, "mission to bring ethical, ecological clothing to the street," and does just that with its urban eco-wear modelled by some of the UK's most influential hip hop and drum and bass artists, including Urban Dub Foundation, Task Force and MC Dynamite. THTC started as Hempology, a hemp awareness group at Hull University, but quickly spread to other campuses and consolidated their vision for a club/music related brand of hemp clothing. With slick finishes and punchy images and slogans – "George Bush & son, family butchers (est. 1989)" and, "Smoke Bush not Afghan" – they're hitting the streetwise market, spreading the hemp word on the urban front line.

Alternatively, for the surfer types, Gekko Bay are your people. From deepest, darkest Cornwall comes the vision of two surfers whose motto is, "If you smoke it you may as well wear it." These hemp designers and producers want to promote and protect the lifestyle they love, "by using hemp fibre to create a more natural approach to clothing and accessories."

Right: Tribal women wearing hemp in Can Cau market, Vietnam.

No wet suits as yet, but perfect casuals to throw on after riding the waves, designed to bring you back down to Earth.

The Hemp Works store in Amsterdam also take their inspiration from the great outdoors and are currently touting the ultimate toking jacket. The Hemp Hoodlamb is warm and water resistant, with a secret stash pocket hidden away in the fur, complemented by the ultimate accessory – a paper dispenser which gives the wearer a rolling paper whenever the need occurs to skin up.

For those whose path has a more pagan twist, there is Spellwear, comfortable hemp cotton mix clothing suitable for yoga, lounging and chillin' with style. The unique feature of these clothes are the spells which are woven into the fabric and embroidered into the tags – wonderful ritual garments ideal for those whose favourite sacrament is that of the sacred smoke. Only you don't want to get hash burns on this clobber. Brainstorm of Aussie Brightonian Catherine Somers, Spellwear is a wonderful weave of warmth and wizardry. The Magician's Housecoat is particularly appealing; embellished with a spell for power, this long luxurious robe is based on the Moroccan Jellaba, and is apparently best worn naked indoors, "to feel the fabric's lushness." Heavenly hemp indeed.

But if you're more Gaultier than guru, there are hemp designs for you too. The big boys and girls of the fashion elite are finally beginning to embrace hemp, and it has apparently become de rigueur in the collections of top designers worldwide. Liz Hancock, Editor of *Project*, an all ethical style magazine, believes that, "This [ethical focus] is going to be fashion's next big trend," and apparently, "People who give a shit are sexy." Katherine Hamnet is forging ahead with her chemical free collection. As part of a practical trial in conjunction with BioRegional, she made a hemp jacket out of the UK's first home produced hemp fabric. The result is a smartly tailored cream pinstripe, modelled amidst luscious hemp vegetation. It's good to wear the green, green grass of home.

But a final note of caution. Wear your weed with pride, be it of urban, outdoor, magical or designer cut, but be aware of the response you may generate. Even with hemp fabrics and fashion making such a powerful comeback after over 70 years of vilification, habits die hard, and the old school might still see your fashion as subversive. Take the case of one American high school student who was weeded out of class for the logo on his t-shirt – Hempstead, NY 516. School staff held on to their 'red flag' even when they were informed that the logo referred to the boy's former hometown of Hempstead on Long Island, New York. "The vigilance of our administrators is important," they bizarrely retorted. There's no talking to some people.

Food, glorious food – or rather hemp, glorious hemp; the plant is one of the most nutritious crops on the planet and virtually a complete food in its own right. The seeds – technically a fruit – are 30-35% oil, mostly the healthy

polyunsaturated variety in a perfect ratio for human consumption. 80% of the oil is made up of essential fatty acids (EFAs), notably the stars of the food world, omega-3 and omega-6 oils. Moreover, another wonder oil, GLA, is also present in hemp seed, placing hemp top of the healthy seed league.

Above: The annual Green Festival in San Francisco promotes hemp use.

Hemp seed oil contains more immunity boosting omega-3 (19-25%) and omega-6 (51-62%) oils than any other, and GLA reduces cholesterol in the body, as well as protecting from

"I don't like people who take drugs... Customs men for example."

Mick Miller, UK stand up comedian.

"I'd like to see the government back a programme of research into the medical properties of cannabis, and I do not object to its responsible use as a recreational relaxant."

Sir Richard Branson, Independent on Sunday, 28 September 1997.

arthritis and PMT. So potent are these EFAs, that researchers are currently working to prove hemp oil's place in the treatment of severely depleted immunity, notably with AIDS patients.

Hemp seeds are also very high in protein (24%) and just a handful provides the adult minimum daily protein requirement in a highly digestible form. These proteins include all eight essential amino acids, which the body cannot manufacture itself, and they are present in a form which is similar to that of blood plasma – i.e. the body doesn't have to work its bollocks off making the food useful; ideal for people convalescing or for those with weakened immunity.

Hemp is fabulous for roughage too, and a handful of seeds in your muesli is a morning must, unless you want go the whole hog and stew up a hearty hemp seed porridge. Seeds can be lightly toasted and tossed in soya sauce for a tasty, high fibre snack, but care needs to be taken, as overheating them means valuable nutrients will be lost and carcinogens created. The rough residue from pressing the seeds for oil is used in animal feeds for fibre and protein. A prolific crop, hemp averages about 55 million seeds per square hectare, and any dropped during harvest are a nutritious favourite for birds.

The seeds can be eaten raw, but more nutrients are released if they are sprouted first,

Left: Detail of a hemp Hmong hill tribe skirt from northern Thailand.

though unfortunately in the US – where, in February 2005, the DEA's attempt to outlaw hemp foods was thrown out by the courts - the seeds are rendered sterile and unsproutable before they are sold. Soak the seeds overnight and then place them in a jar on its side with the lid off. Rinse them twice a day and eat when the shoots are 5-10mm long. Soaking and sprouting breaks down the protective layers within the seeds, making them easily digested. Scattered on a salad and drizzled with nutty hemp oil, they create a power packed meal. Alternatively, sprouted seeds can be blended with fruit, juice or yoghurt to make a hemp smoothie. Another drink - green hemp milk – is created by blending the sprouted seeds with cannabis leaves and water or soya milk to make a creamy green drink. Cheers!

Hemp oil can be used in any cooking, but it's quite expensive and is altered by heating. As with the seeds, overheating affects hemp oil's chemical structure and dangerous carcinogenic free radicals can be created.

More gourmet than gruel, hemp seeds and oil lend themselves to hundreds of tempting recipes and ready made meals. Like soya products, hemp can be made into a vegan milk, texturised for veggie meat alternatives, made into porridge, hemp seed butter, roasted and pressed into breads and cakes... the list is endless. There are plenty of hemp cook books out there for any budding chefs to get creative with this wonder food.

But a quick word of warning for the over enthusiastic. For a psychotropic snack use the bud. If you run out of stash leave that jar of seeds from the health shop well alone – there's no THC in the seeds and if you eat too many, you might end up shitting yourself – not out of stoned paranoia – but because your chosen stash would equal two or three strong doses of high fibre laxative! Pass the bog roll please.

Hemp in the bathroom – lotions, potions and all things body beautiful

In a nutshell, hemp is wonderful for your skin and hair. So long as it is not simply being used as a trendy selling point in an otherwise pollutant packed potion, hemp is really one of the best products you can use on your body. Simply soak and then grind hemp seeds for an invigorating and nourishing exfoliant. There are tons of pot products in the ever expanding market for specific beauty benefits, but are there any facts to back up the claims?

Hemp's beauty secrets are locked away in its seeds. Pressed into oil, it is the basis of all hemp beauty products for skin and hair, and a valuable remedy in itself. The essential fatty acids (EFAs), – while so good for us to eat – are equally beneficial when applied to the skin. They are readily absorbed into the body, deeply nourishing the various layers of the skin as they go. It's all thanks to those omega-3 and -6 oils, GLAs and essential amino acids.

Hemp is the superior beauty oil for the same reasons that it is the most complete food oil - it is the only one that is high in EFAs, GLAs and essential amino acids. This makes it easily absorbed and very adept at maintaining a healthy balance of lipids and moisture in the skin. Hemp oil can help alleviate skin conditions such as atopic eczema, psoriasis and acne with its anti-inflammatory ability, which also helps with minor cuts and broken skin.

Hemp oil really helps aging skin as well. Healthy young skin contains plenty of essential fatty acids, proteins and lipids, which prevent excessive water loss. As skin gets older, its metabolism slows, resulting in a drop in natural EFA levels. Hemp oil on the skin can partially compensate for this drop in EFA and help maintain a softer, better lubricated complexion.

So there's a fair bit of science behind hemp's claim to space in the bathroom cabinet. Whilst many beauty products boast high levels of EFAs, the only ones which have been biochemically and therapeutically proven to make a difference are omega-6, omega-3 and GLA, all of which exist in an abundant balance in hemp.

And there is a flourishing hemp beauty industry to prove it, as evidenced by the success of companies like The Body Shop and Dr. Bronner's. Estimated at $5 million in 1993, the market soared to $150 million by 1999. But when it comes to hemp, beauty is more than skin deep. The vast majority of hemp beauty products are ecologically sound too, beautifying the planet with cannabis sativa so the bathroom cabinets can stay well stocked.

Cannabis, the wonder weed, can be eaten, drunk, worn, washed with, lived in, driven and, of course, smoked. But what use can hemp be when we need to go to the loo? Well, apart from the possibility of good old hemp bog roll, there is a bigger picture. Not only would the use of industrial hemp massively reduce greenhouse gasses, and not only does the plant re-oxygenate our suffering atmosphere, but it makes a great mop up crop for human effluent. Keith Bolton, Project Manager of Southern Cross University's Ecotechnology Research Centre in Australia, had the novel idea of planting his one hectare crop of hemp on a pile of human excrement at a sewerage treatment plant. Within 100 days he had produced 18 tonnes of top class industrial hemp, and mopped up 10 million litres of effluent. Can't complain about that, you would imagine, unless, of course, you are one of the illegal growers downwind of his field.

If you smoked an entire paddock of Dr Bolton's crop you would get a headache rather than a high, and serious smokers are worried that his low THC strains will contaminate their high THC crops. His shit isn't good shit, it's shit shit, but as Dr Bolton concluded, "I think that we will just have to learn to co-exist."

Right: Chinese Tip-top Miao girls in traditional cannabis costume.

Chapter 4

Far Out Films

Cinema's relationship with weed has been no less erratic than any other medium. Whenever it has been politically or commercially viable, marijuana has been wheeled out as an appropriate whipping boy, prime for exploitation.

Far out Films

The earliest of these so called public information films were made at the beginning of the 20th century, and primarily dealt with addictions to harder drugs, such as opiates and amphetamines. Subtle titles like *The Accursed Drug* and *Slave of Morphine*, both made in 1913, and *The Devil's Needle* in 1916 shocked and intrigued the public. Hollywood censors were already aware of the power of this relatively new medium and were acutely conscious that films could be both a force for good and bad. Unsurprisingly perhaps, these forces exist in an uneasy balance to the present day, both needing each other to support their own opposing ends – saving lost souls and making tons of cash.

While America was gripped in the Prohibition era – after the temperance movement managed to outlaw alcohol when the Volstead Act was passed in 1919 – Hollywood began to get to grips with self regulation. On March 7 1921, The Association of The Motion Picture Industry issued the first edict against depictions of drug use in films. It advised against films that had, "Stories which make gambling and drunkenness attractive, or scenes which show the use of narcotics and other unnatural practices dangerous to social morality."

Until the 1920s, marijuana was rarely featured in US films and was constantly misrepresented. Directors' poor research often confused the most well known form of marijuana – hashish – and its effects, with those of opium, tarnishing cannabis with a harder reputation than it deserved. For a brief time, a series of 1920s' films created a bizarre sub-genre – the Marijuana Cowboy Western. Regularly referred to as 'locoweed' or 'Jimson weed', marijuana's effects were deliberately distorted for dramatic impact. *Notch Number One* (1924) had cowboys getting high, violent and then committing murder, rather than sitting around eating Doritos and watching cartoons. The imaginatively entitled *High on the Range* (1929) told the story of Chick, a dope smoking 'desert weakling' who passes dope out to all his pardners. One of them finally snaps on the weed, and shoots his old rancher boss after losing his job for kicking horses.

Above: The 1920s' alcohol prohibition was just as effective as today's cannabis ban.

In 1922, the former US Postmaster General, Will Hays, concerned with the subject matter that directors were choosing to focus on – i.e. sex, drugs and lewd music – produced a list of 'Don'ts and Be Carefuls' for the film industry. It listed 36 topics that should be avoided or handled with extreme care if Hollywood wanted to avert censorship. These included the obvious stuff about sex, violence and, "The illegal traffic of drugs, the use of drugs and methods of smuggling." Unsurprisingly, the majority of the studios pretty much ignored Hays' list, and continued to wheel out one torrid tale after another.

Eight years later, in 1930, Hollywood finally realized something had to be done to control the excesses of film makers, and so the industry adopted the more rigid Motion Picture Production Code. The Code quite clearly stated that the drug trade should be covered up. It stipulated, "Illegal drug traffic must *never* be represented," and, "Because of its evil consequences, the drug traffic should *never* be presented in any form. The existence of the trade should not be brought to the attention of audiences." Despite this, it still took a major boycott of cinemas - over sexual imagery – by the powerful Catholic Legion of Decency in 1934, for the strict enforcement of the Code to take place.

Any film found to be in breach of the Code had its distribution severely limited. The film would fail to be issued a seal of approval, which meant that most first run cinemas, owned by the big studios, refused to show them as they faced a $25,000 fine.

However, there were small independent theatres, art houses, black cinemas and grind houses that were willing to take non-seal films. Independent B-movie distributors (many from carnival backgrounds) began touring their films around America, and the golden age of exploitation began. Many would simply turn up in a town, set up a big tent and screen their movies for a week before rolling on.

One of the chief evangelists of these sleaze-o-rama spectaculars was Dwain Esper, exploitationist extraordinaire. Esper's entire career hung on maintaining the drugs hysteria and fear that swept America from the Thirties to the Fifties. A fear mostly generated thanks to his movies. His first as producer and director was *Narcotic* in 1932, which told of a dope addicted doctor who ends up as a snake oil salesman, and ultimately descends into depression and commits suicide. A jolly tale loosely based on his uncle in law.

1932 was also the year that Harry J Anslinger became Director of the newly formed Federal Bureau of Narcotics (the forerunner to the Drug Enforcement Agency). Anslinger became cannabis' arch-nemesis and he sought to eradicate it from the American consciousness with an almost fanatical zeal.

Esper however, could see an ally in Anslinger, as the latter preached his fervent anti-pot sermon from the pulpit of the press and in numerous speeches on the inherent evils of the plant.

In 1935, Anslinger purportedly gave his blessing and assistance to Esper's sensational marijuana expose, *Assassin of Youth*. In it is told the familiar story of a high school girl introduced to weed, who is quickly sucked into the criminal underworld, wild parties and unbridled passions. Once she has been sufficiently degraded and humiliated, a disguised reporter smashes the dope fiends' ring. The simplistic morality and highly inaccurate depictions of cannabis use and its effects were fast becoming the staple diet for exploitational drug films. But the public didn't care, they lapped it up. So, Esper, keen to please his audience, quickly released *Marihuana – Weed With Roots in Hell*. The trailer promised cinema goers would, "See marihuana unfolding new pitfalls for America's youth." Esper and Anslinger's principal propaganda ploy was always to put the fear into parents about how cannabis was corrupting children. Yet in all of Esper's films, it's hard to find an actor who appears to be under 35, let alone a youth.

1936 saw Esper acquire the rights to *Tell Your Children*, an anti-cannabis melodrama produced by an LA church group. It hadn't done much business until Esper worked his marketing magic and re-titled it *Reefer Madness*, creating one of the great cult drug movies of all time. With hindsight, the film is more than a little risible, with over the top, ham acting that would make a pig cringe. But people were less informed in

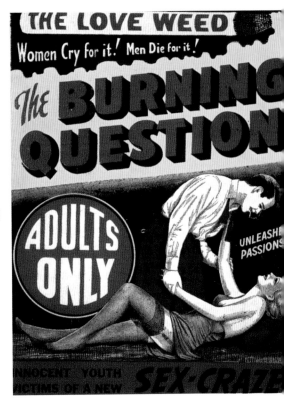

Above: *Reefer Madness* was re-released in America under several different names including *The Burning Question* and *Doped Youth*.

1936, and there was a genuine fear generated by this unbalanced anti-pot propaganda.

Anslinger and his cronies finally got their way in 1937, when the US Congress passed the Marijuana Tax Act, the first federal legislation regulating the cultivation and sale of cannabis. The Tax Act effectively suppressed any kind of discussion that might arise about the legal and moral usage of cannabis within the media, and it dropped off the radar as a topic for directors.

Then, with America's involvement in World War Two, the government flipped a 180 degree turn that would make any stoner's head spin. In 1942, Japan had effectively cut off the main trading route for rope and paper from the Philippines, so in a complete reversal of policy, the US government actively encouraged farmers to grow cannabis with the propaganda film, *Hemp for Victory*. The Agricultural department distributed 400,000lbs of cannabis seeds to farmers from Wisconsin to Kentucky and made them watch the film, which featured fields of marijuana plants. With hindsight, the enormous hypocrisy of the government is laid bare.

The Second World War also saw a change of villain, when it came to the corrupters of American youth. No longer were Negroes and Mexicans to blame, instead it was fifth columnist Nazis luring America's children astray with reefers. Films such as J D Kendis' 1941 *Devil's*

Left: The exploitation films often fuelled parents' unfounded fears for their kids.

Harvest helped perpetuate the myth. The reality was that Nazi Germany's spy ring was practically crushed before it began.

In 1947, 17 years after it was introduced, The Motion Picture Production Code still clearly stated that, "The illegal drug must not be portrayed in such a way as to stimulate curiosity, nor shall scenes be approved which show the use of illegal drugs, or their effects in detail." However, all that was about to change thanks to Harry Anslinger. The head of the Federal Bureau of Narcotics had extreme delusions of grandeur when he gave Bureau assistance, and even acted in, *To The Ends of the Earth*, in 1947. This all action, globetrotting thriller about drug busting agents was given a seal of approval. Hollywood saw the chink in the Code's armour and went for blood. Before the Code's administrators knew it, more and more films were slipping under the loophole Anslinger had ironically helped to create.

That same year saw the biggest Hollywood drugs scandal in 25 years. Major movie star Robert Mitchum was arrested for possession of marijuana, while smoking at the home of blonde starlet Lila Leeds. It was the equivalent of Tom Cruise mainlining heroin, while having sex with a crack whore in the middle of Times Square. Mitchum rightly thought his career and marriage were over. But, after serving 60 days in an open prison, he emerged unscathed and continued a successful career. Lila Leeds wasn't so lucky.

After serving time, her MGM contract was dropped and she was forced on to the B-movie circuit. Kroger Babb, an exploitationist in the vein of Esper, put Leeds in the snappily titled, *She Shoulda Said No – But She Didn't*. Sam Newfield directed the film, understandably under the alias of Sherman Scott. Babb soon shortened the title to the more market friendly *Wild Weed*, or *Devil's Weed*, as it was also known. It was the familiar story of good girl gone bad thanks to too many tokes on a joint. As with so many of these over dramatised morality plays, cannabis was always the thin end of the wedge, invariably leading to harder drugs, degradation, madness and finally death. Despite, or perhaps because of this, the film proved so popular it continued to get theatrical release right into the Fifties.

But the North Americans didn't have a monopoly on marijuana movies. Argentinean director León Klimovsky's own take on *Marihuana*, in 1950, was a Spanish ethics tale about Dr Pablo Urioste, a respected surgeon, played by Pedro López Lagar. Urioste is forced into a nightmarish twilight world after his wife, a marijuana 'addict', dies at a nightclub. He recounts his story to the police – of how he is hooked, beaten, blackmailed, and even throws in some bad trip flashbacks for good measure.

Meanwhile, back in the USA, Dwain Esper was still churning out his tosh. In 1955 he released *The Pusher*, under his Social Service Pictures banner. Esper was getting desperate by now and was cannibalising his early films. Large portions of his 1936 flick, *Marijuana – Weed With Roots in Hell*, were erratically cut into *The Pusher* and the hammy acting stood out like a sore thumb, even to a Fifties' audience. The clips were erroneously credited as, "Re-enacted case histories taken from the files of narcotic enforcement agencies." After numerous cases where dope smoking teenagers predictably meet sticky ends, the narrator warns, "If you should ever be confronted with the temptation of taking that first puff of a marijuana cigarette, DON'T DO IT! Turn away from it as you would to avoid the most poisonous snake, for it is a thousand times more deadly!"

By the 1960s though, the Code was finally losing any vestige of relevance. Increasingly, producers and directors were rebelling against the aesthetic and moral straightjacket it imposed. Less rigid attitudes to sex, more tolerance, intellectual curiosity, and less willingness to bend to Christian dogmas, all contributed to the Code's demise. As the Sixties wound its winding way, the love generation were switched on to more powerful drugs like LSD and magic mushrooms, and with their minds freed (or mashed – depending on your point of view), they questioned their parents' moral standpoints regarding drug use.

It was LSD's turn to be demonised on the silver screen and cannabis breathed a minor sigh of relief.

Right: Marijuana scare films were usually an excuse for salacious scenes with 'corrupted' girls.

Personal Highs:
Air America

Many smokers nowadays score from secret gardeners. But when local weed is in short supply how does cheap marijuana get into the USA? Through thousands of secret flights from Mexico, is how. One pilot, 'Sky Six', spilled the beans on the www.budlife420.com website back in 2002.

"I was a 'fly by the seat of my pants' crop duster pilot risking my life flying under and over high voltage power lines, inhaling pesticides when the wind changed, and flying only a few feet over crops. The pay was good, but the life expectancy for a crop dusting pilot was bad. Few lived more than 10 years. I had a friend who had just cut his crop duster through some power lines and crashed, ending his career. It was at this friend's funeral that I was recruited to take his place, flying in loads of marijuana from Mexico.

"A few days later, I went to a dirt road used as a landing strip. The plane, a stripped down Cessna 185 'Skywagon', was waiting for me. My flying and fuelling instructions for Mexico were all I was told; the rest of the instructions were to be given to me by some man with a gold tooth outside of Culiacan, Mexico… I didn't even know the names of these guys and I felt stupid trusting them. Anyway, they paid me $2,000 advance money for expenses and I took off.

"The trip one way was about 1,200 miles. The fuel stops on the trip down were all at small, out of the way airports. I had been given a suitcase full of cash to buy the load of marijuana and I had my advance of $2,000 expense money for fuel and small bribes.

"Arriving outside of Culiacan, I sighted the dirt road and landed. Two old, rusty pickup trucks and some short red and brown skinned men wearing white, straw cowboy hats were waiting for me. All of them had rifles or shotguns. The boss came up to the plane and greeted me with one of his front teeth capped in gold, glistening in the hot sun. He smiled, shook my hand and examined the empty plane, 'Do you have the cash?' I handed him the suitcase with the load money… The plane was fuelled and the 800 pounds of cloth sacks full of marijuana bricks were loaded into the plane. 'Sometimes we have five or six planes a day refuelling at the Hermosillo Airport,' said the gold toothed boss. I knew this was a big operation, an 'Air Force of smugglers' bringing in marijuana to the US.

"At Hermosillo Airport, I was greeted by uniformed guards, who directed the fuelling. They never looked at anything as I gave them a $50 bill. I knew they smelled the load of marijuana but it was ignored. I got some coffee, stretched my legs, paid the fuel bill, and was back in the air in 20 minutes.

"It was getting light now as I approached the Arizona border… I had to stay below radar detection on this unregistered, illegal international flight or suspicions would be aroused.

"Finally, I arrived back at the farm where I had

They never looked at anything as I gave them a $50 bill. I knew they smelled the load of marijuana but it was ignored.

started. Including my expense money, I had worked two days straight for $6,000 cash. I had made about two months' pay in two days. I was paid the balance of my cash while the sacks full of marijuana bricks were unloaded from the plane. While this was a successful trip, it stressed me out too much and I knew I wouldn't be doing this again anytime soon. $10,000 cash would have enticed me, but not the $6,000 that I made.

"I finally tried smoking marijuana, as the Mexican stranger had given me one brick as a bonus. I still do smoke on occasion. I did my part as a smuggler and paid my dues. Now I'm a 65 year old man and I'll tell you one thing, if the BS laws prohibiting marijuana were changed, nobody would waste their time taking risks flying in marijuana the way I did."

So now you know. Buy local!

1967's *Mary Jane*, starring popstar Fabian, tried to open up the debate again over legalization by using the same old scare tactics of the Thirties and a more 'with it' slant, but it was woefully out of step with the times. Smoking cannabis in films became more of an accepted act for characters who weren't fallen or sleazy, and the general tone became more humorous than sanctimonious. As the new counterculture swept the States, the major studios tried cashing in with comedies such as the Peter Sellers 1968 vehicle, *I Love You, Alice B Toklas*. The title refers to the pioneering cook who wrote *the* book on cooking with cannabis, and the uplifting pro-pot film tells of a lawyer who drops out of the rat race after discovering LSD and hash brownies.

The concern over excessive drug use in the Sixties caused the establishment to create numerous educational films including *Marijuana*, also in 1968. This had nothing to do with Esper's 1936 film, but was no less hilarious. In it, a gold lamé pyjama-ed Sonny Bono raps to the kids about the dangers of booze, pot and pills with the usual scaremonger stories about chicks driving off cliffs while tripping out on the beauty of nature, Daddy-O. Tragically, Bono looks completely whacked out on drugs himself, and has the credibility of an alcoholic saying, "Don't drink and drive," as he tears down the motorway into oncoming traffic at 90 mph. Other films made specifically to warn high school students about the drug menace included *World of Weed* (1968),

Above: Peter Sellers as a hippie stoner convert in *I Love You Alice B Toklas*.

Right: Leigh Taylor-Young sparks one up in the same film.

Spliffs 3

Marijuana: The Great Escape (1970), *The Story of Marijuana* (1971), and endless others with the word 'marijuana' in it. But, of course, cannabis users were invariably better informed than the film makers, and there was growing concern that the films were actually having the opposite to the intended effect; switching audiences ON to drugs, not off.

Another area of educational films was the more restricted movies made for the police, army and medical personnel. These disinformation exercises simply spouted the government's continued anti-cannabis maxim. In 1970's *The People Vs Pot*, cannabis is presented as addictive, a stepping stone to harder drugs and capable of triggering 'the killer instinct.' All facts that, today, are tenuous at best.

As the Seventies rolled on, old scaremonger classics like *Reefer Madness* were rediscovered by late night art house cinemas and played for laughs to a more informed audience. These films toured the college campuses as they were now in the public domain. Esper desperately tried to squeeze one last cent out of his flicks, but failed and died broke in 1982.

More acceptance of 'soft' drugs meant the time was right for stand up stoner comedians, Cheech Marin and Tommy Chong, to hit the big screen. For years they'd been successfully doing the club circuit, and their first album, in 1971, went gold.

Right: "It's mostly Maui Wowie, but it's got some Labrador in it."

"Marijuana makes fiends of boys in 30 days; hashish goads users to blood lust."

Hearst newspaper headline, 1936.

"Casual drug users should be taken out and shot."

Darryl Gates, ex-Head of Los Angeles
Police Department, United States, before
a Senate Judiciary Committee, 1990.

Seven years later they made what became a stoner classic, cult comedy movie, *Up in Smoke*. Cheech and Chong's film was jam packed with drugs references and jokes. It was the complete antithesis of any previous major Hollywood studio movie, actually revelling in the stoner counterculture, as it told the tale of two wasters who inadvertently smuggle a van made entirely of marijuana over the Mexican border. Desperate to score throughout the film, they are blissfully unaware that they are driving a massive bale of grass around LA, or even that the Narcs are following them.

The film was such a hit that Cheech and Chong followed up it with numerous others in a similar vein, including *Nice Dreams* (1981), *Things are Tough All Over* (1982) and *Still Smoking* (1983). In fact, the stoner Laurel and Hardy made seven movies between 1978 and 1985. Their last film together as the stoned duo was *Get Out of My Room* in 1985. It was a mock-u-mentry featuring parts of their stand up routines. However, the two have made guest appearances in various films and television programmes including the controversial cartoon, *South Park*. Since Tommy Chong's arrest for selling bongs, the two have reformed their friendship after a prolonged estrangement, and there are rumours of a new Cheech and Chong movie on the horizon. No bad thing, as their films have inspired and influenced a whole stoner generation.

Cannabis and comedy are natural buddies, so it's not surprising that there have been more comedies about grass than any other genre. Cheech and Chong helped pave the way for films such as Mel Brooks' *The History of the World Part I* to joke about weed. In the 1981 comedy, Brooks and Gregory Hines are being chased by the Roman army when they discover, "a whole field of wacky baccy." After demanding some, "rolling papyrus", Hines' character rolls an enormous joint which gets the centurions stoned and leaves the heroes free to escape!

Then there's rapper Ice Cube's 1995 comedy, *Friday*. It's a day in the life of a pair of African American youths in South Central LA. Cube plays Craig, a frustrated teen who suffers the ultimate humiliation of being fired on his day off. The then unknown Chris Tucker plays Smokey, a marijuana lovin' homeboy whose passion for the green stuff lands him in predicament after predicament. Not least of which is the fact he was given $200 worth of weed to sell by the local dealer, which he ended up smoking instead, and if he can't come up with the money by the end of the day, he'll be in a world of hurt. This 'dudes in trouble thanks to grass' mcguffin was also the key plot to 1998's *Half-Baked*. When Kenny accidentally kills a cop's diabetic horse by feeding it the food he purchased from a munchie run, he is put in jail and is given a $1 million bail. His buddies try to bail him out by selling marijuana

Right: Cheech and Chong enjoy some *Nice Dreams* in their 1981 movie.

that one of them gets through his job as a janitor at a pharmaceutical lab. The film features a ton of cameos from pro-legalization stars including comedian Steven Wright, actors Stephen Baldwin and Janeane Garofalo, musicians Snoop Dogg and Willie Nelson and, of course, the godfather of ganja comedy, Tommy Chong.

But while many films still focus on young dudes getting into stoner scrapes, such as Richard Linklater's affectionate look at Seventies' teenagers in *Dazed and Confused* (1993), there has been a broadening of who is portrayed actually smoking cannabis. In *Saving Grace* (2000), a 'respectable' middle aged widow (played by Brenda Blethyn) gets high with her gardener (played by Craig Ferguson who co-wrote the film) and grows grass in her orchid greenhouse to help her out of a financial crisis. The whole village, including the local police constable, is well aware of the endeavour and is hoping for their success.

And of course who could forget those other prodigious growers of weed in 1998's *Lock, Stock and Two Smoking Barrels*?

Winston: Just make sure if you do need to buy sodding fertilizer to be a bit more subtle.
Willie: What do you mean?
Winston: We grow copious amounts of ganja, yah. And you're carrying a wasted girl and a bag of fertilizer. You don't look like your average horti-fucking-culturalist!

The public school growers get completely out of their depth when heavily armed East End gangsters decide to raid the heavily fortified hydroponic haven and relieve them of their crop.

With a more balanced and realistic attitude to cannabis portrayal on the silver screen, many new documentary makers began to redress the imbalance caused by the exploitational films of the Thirties. In 1997, former *High Times* Editor Ed Rosenthal produced and starred in *Cannabis Rising*, an excellent 30 minute documentary which gave a behind the scenes look at the Coffee Shops, Cannabis Castle and Mega-Grow Rooms of Holland. *High Times* magazine commented that the film, "comes across as an enticing promotional tour from some imaginary marijuana tourist bureau." Another excellent documentary made a few years later, in 1999, was Ron Mann's *Grass*. Narrated by actor Woody Harrelson it relates the tragi-comic story of the 'War on Drugs' and in particular, the reasons why weed went out of the legal window.

Released to only a handful of cinemas in the spring of 1998, *Homegrown* was neglected by nervous distributors who couldn't work out how to market a movie about marijuana farmers. As a result, hardly anyone saw this *Fargo*-esque comedy thriller about three experienced pot growers in northern California (Billy Bob

Right: The stoner heroes of *Half-Baked* find a novel way of getting high.

The emperor of hemp

The idea that a one time member of the military police and pro-war Republican prohibitionist could become the leader of the pro-hemp movement, writer of the most famous book on marijuana, and even get a strain of weed named after him, may sound like a tall tale told by a stoner, but this is exactly what happened to Jack Herer.

Born in Brooklyn in 1939, Herer was a typical American nerd of the type often lampooned in Hollywood movies. He worked in sign maintenance and had little knowledge of marijuana or hemp in any of its guises. This all changed when he was 30 years old and a girlfriend wanted to introduce him to a new experience, "She tried three times to get me high. Finally it worked, and I had the most incredible sex I'd ever had. My first words after orgasm were, 'This is illegal?' I couldn't believe it." Herer saw a new life as a marijuana activist and author unfold before him.

Herer is not just a 'Hey, everybody should be allowed to have a toke...' kind of guy. He firmly believes that widespread use of hemp will save

Above: Jack Herer (left) and fellow activist Captain Ed Adair.

the planet – a strong position to take these days, even as evidence mounts that mankind is destroying natural resources at an unsustainable rate. You see, a good bit of weed can do way more than get you high; it can be used to produce paper, fibre, fuel, oil, textiles and could stem the tide of deforestation. It is the most sustainable crop on the planet, growing everywhere from the Arctic to the equator, up on high mountains to low lying plains. And its growth helps replenish the land like no other plant, thanks to a root system which breaks up the soil to a great depth.

The reasons that marijuana and hemp are illegal in the US are complex and Machiavellian, but it has little to do with the fact that it makes people high. Herer's research into the history of the plant and its subsequent outlawing reveals that much of the push to criminalize the plant's growth came from paper manufacturers and petrochemical companies.

It was facts such as these that led him to write possibly the most famous book on marijuana, *The Emperor Wears No Clothes*. In it, he outlines the history of cannabis and hemp, going into great detail regarding its use around the world in many different guises. Yet its use has virtually been scrapped from our history books as it is painted as a demonic scourge on society. Nobody mentions that you could be arrested in America at one time for NOT growing it, or that British citizenship used to be granted only to those who would grow hemp. But it wasn't the

history of cannabis that set him writing in 1982. It was his firm belief that a return to its use would greatly reduce our reliance on polluting chemicals, "You see, the Greenhouse Effect is a direct result of burning fossil or old carbon fuels. There is only one plant that can completely substitute for fossil fuel. The plant is an annual that grows in all 50 States. It is the fastest growing sustainable biomass on the planet." He was, of course, referring to our favourite 'weed'.

Since writing *The Emperor Wears No Clothes*, Herer has been a vocal campaigner for hemp to be taken seriously. Unfortunately, not everyone takes him seriously. When he approached Steve Rawlings, the highest ranking official in the US Department of Agriculture, and the man charged with reversing the Greenhouse Effect, he realized just what he was up against. Asked what would be the best way of reversing the Greenhouse Effect, Rawlings replied, "Stop cutting down trees and stop using fossil fuels." The only way we can do this is if we find something else to use instead, and so Herer presented the case for hemp. Rawlings saw the logic and agreed that the plant would do the job well, but wanted to point out to Herer that hemp is also marijuana, and therefore illegal.

"Well, you know marijuana's illegal, don't you? You can't use it."

Herer replied, "Not even to save the world?"

"No. It's illegal," he was informed. "You cannot use something illegal."

Since then, tolerance for such arguments has fallen even further in the US, and is currently at an all time low. Some would say it's because of George W Bush's continuing war on drugs, but most believe it is because of his involvement and fortunes made in petrochemicals, the industry that would suffer most if widespread use of hemp was reintroduced.

In 1995, a strain of marijuana carrying the name Jack Herer won the annual Cannabis Cup in Amsterdam. It is an incredibly strong smoke, with an immediate and cerebral high, and a popular favourite with visitors to the city's coffee shops. However, to really honour Herer we all need to wake up to the fact that hemp has so much more to offer than a good buzz. We need to point out to the politicians that they are wrong, and if they disagree we need to remove them from power and replace them with people who represent the views and needs of the public and planet – not of the petrochemical companies.

That's what Herer would want us to do. His web site (www.jackherer.com) offers $100,000 to anyone who can prove his research wrong. It also has online copies of his book and writings, plus a draft amendment to America's laws regarding cannabis, detailing how they must change. His isn't just a fight to get high, but a fight to save the planet. So roll yourself a big fat one, and join the crusade.

Above: The book that sparked the 1980s' pro-legalization resurgence.

Thornton, Hank Azaria – of *The Simpsons* – and Ryan Phillippe) who guard their valuable outdoor crop against raids by the cops and unwanted competitors. When their boss is murdered, Thornton assumes the dead man's identity to arrange one last, lucrative deal, but pulling off the scam proves to be much harder than they'd thought (doesn't it always?). The three potheads routinely get high on their own supply as *Homegrown* turns into a taut thriller fuelled in equal parts by comedy and paranoid tension. Like *Half-Baked*, the pro-pot stars came out in support, with big name cameos including Jamie Lee Curtis, Ted Danson, and John Lithgow. But despite all this, it still failed to find an audience. It's safe to say that while the Code is no longer functioning, the fear factor still hangs heavy over Hollywood, and so the movie fell victim to the misguided belief that any portrayal of drugs and illegal activity is still considered promotion of such.

However, the flower children of the Sixties and Seventies have grown up and, now integrated into the mass media, continue their benign propaganda campaign for cannabis use. This generation created one of the most successful pro-cannabis cartoon series of all time, *The Simpsons*. At the end of one episode the police

Left: Ellen Barber and John Lithgow in 1972's *Dealing*, based on Michael Crichton's novel.

raid a blind man's house and discover a small packet of dope, "This is for medical purposes, right?" asks police chief Wiggum. "Er… right!" comes the reply. The police stay, get stoned and party. In another episode, Homer discovers some old junk in the attic including a bong and recalls, "I haven't seen one of these for years. Far out, man." They even named one segment of a *Treehouse of Horror* episode, *Reaper Madness*, in honour of Dwain Esper.

This not so subliminal pro-cannabis stand culminated in the episode *Weekend at Burnsies*. Homer gets addicted to medical marijuana when it is prescribed for a pain in his eye and when he learns that medicinal marijuana is going to be outlawed in his State, he campaigns erratically for pro-pot legalization. *The Simpsons'* writers walk a fine line, avoiding demonizing the weed but aware of the pitfalls, thus giving a humorous but balanced portrayal of the effects of smoking grass. For example, when Marge asks Homer where has he been he replies, "Whoa! One question at a time! Yes, you?" and the immortal line, "We have a kitchen?"

But in the UK, restrictions have been loosened even more, not only on the reclassification of marijuana, but also on it's TV portrayal. Alternative comedy shows like *Spaced* and *Shameless* have characters constantly skinning up and smoking cannabis, without any comment. The recent BBC 3 comedy, starring stand up Johnny Vegas, *Ideal*, takes the concept one stage further by casting him as Moz, an actual cannabis

dealer (I deal – clever, eh?). Moz is a small time hash dealer who lives in a run down bedsit in Manchester with his long term girlfriend Nicki. Moz is a low achiever, and quite happy with it, but Nicki has aspirations of a better life. The series takes place entirely in Moz's flat, with an array of customers and misfits passing through his life on a daily basis. Moz deals only in marijuana and sees himself as providing a crucial service to the community, and Vegas obviously has a soft spot for his character, "I think Moz is a dealer who has a bit of a conscience, really. He's very strict in that he won't deal anything other than hash and weed, which doesn't make him very successful as a dealer. He doesn't seem to make much money from it and you don't see him with anything of value."

Both the big and small screens have come a long way from the didactic fire and brimstone movies of the Thirties. The media now integrates pot smoking wherever it is relevant without the need for moralizing or huge warnings. Whether this trend continues, remains to be seen. One thing though, is for certain. Despite the fact that marijuana and the media sometimes make odd bed fellows, they'll maintain their symbiotic relationship – for better or for worse – for some time to come.

Right: Ali G at the premiere of his movie with a bevy of 'budding' beauties.

Chapter 5

Festival Freak Out!

Everyone knows it's more fun smoking a bud with buds, and where's better to share than at a festival, trade show or gathering? Not only can you find the latest in smoking technology, but you can trade growing tips, pick up some cool hemp products and, of course, share a few spliffs.

Festival freak out!

Nearly all cannabis related events are either typical outdoor hippie fests with live bands singing about the green, green grass of home, or more prosaic trade fairs held in traditional conference halls (and even the latter have their 'subversive' edge, with stallholders offering hits from their bongs!).

Whatever the event, one thing that unifies them is a strong campaigning element, with many raising money for various reform charities, all desperately trying to change the law.

However, it's not all about being 'worthy'. A good time can be found at nearly all the shows, festies and events, and with them happening all over the world, it's quite possible to travel the globe in a happy, heady haze of hemp. From the UK to the USA, Australia to Holland, there's a festival, march, rally or fair happening practically every weekend somewhere on the planet. So, for the connoisseur looking to celebrate their favourite plant, here's a brief guide to just a few of the vast array of events on offer.

The Cannabis Cup

Let's face it, the Dutch know how to put on a sensimilla show. Well, they've had more practice than anyone else. As any stoner knows, the semi-mythical Cannabis Cup is held in Amsterdam every year, attracting consumers, cultivators and campaigners from around the world. Its origins lie back in the smoky mists of time and several people are credited with starting it. Some claim it was legendary writer/campaigner Ed Rosenthal who, armed with just $600, created a big party for stoners that just kept on growing. Others would claim that Steven Hager launched the Cup in 1987. Either way, both men worked for *High Times* magazine, and the publication has been an integral part of the five day event ever since. Growers, coffee shops and dealers all vie for the prestigious awards that can mean the difference between ticking over as a cottage business, and full blown commercial success (despite the fact that they have to pay to enter their wares in the competition).

Above: The sexy spirit of sensimilla will open your consciousness' third eye.

The majority of the event takes place at the Pax Party House near the Heineken Brewery, on the edge of the city. There are lectures, discussions and insane smoking competitions as well as a massive trade fair full of semi-clad ladies. Buds and babes galore. Toking tourists are then driven on a tour of coffee shops until they can smoke no more, before retiring to the Melkweg nightclub to chill.

Highlife Hemp Fair

But there's another, equally important 'rival' show in Holland. The Highlife Hemp Fair, held at the Utrecht Exhibition Centre, covers over 12,000 metres and was instigated by the sharp dressed, constantly mobile using, Boy Ramsahai. This slick entrepreneur is head of an empire which began with the Dutch magazine *Highlife* in 1990, and which is now at the cutting edge of cannabis culture. *Highlife*'s fair started in 1997 and has grown from a trestle table market to a real trade show filled with businessmen in suits on mobile phones teaching seminars on credit sales and production relocation. The Turkish press described the fair as a cross between an agricultural exhibition and a motor show, punctuated with bikini-clad women delivering company prospectuses. Even so, the smell of weed is pervasive and passive smoking is enjoyed by all.

An impressive 13,000 people turned up in 2004, making the Highlife Hemp fair one of

Left: True stoners don't sit on the fence, but wear their beliefs on their sleeves. Or in this case a T-shirt.

Right: A tokin' tourist enjoys a pipe in The Greenhouse coffee shop in Amsterdam, during the Cannabis Cup.

the most successful cannabis trade shows. The highlight of the Highlife show is the presentation of the Cup for the best weed and hash from Holland. If the Cannabis Cup is the stoner's Oscar, then The Highlife Cup is the BAFTA.

While many hark back to the days when the Fair was more fun and was an intimate gathering of radical spirits baying for change, the new look event reflects the revolution that has seized the hemp industry in recent years. All things hemp have become the biggest growth area of the Dutch economy, with a turnover of 5-10 billion Euros annually, accounting for 1-2% of the Dutch GDP – way above the high profile tulip and cut flower industry.

But many exhibitors still tread a fine line with the law. At the 2004 show, Bryon Sheppard, from British Columbia in Canada, brought his fully automated plant boxes for indoor production. He puts flowers in the boxes when he exhibits in the US, "But the connoisseurs know that you can grow other things apart from roses and tomatoes [in them]," he said slyly.

In 2005, the Mayor of Utrecht threatened to close the fair down, leading to a ban on the distribution of free samples. Instead, punters were given free beer in an attempt to keep up the Highlife reputation for a relaxed party atmosphere in the big bad world of cannabis commerce. Which perhaps seems to defeat the main objective of the show, but who's

"I can envisage a new world in which society has a way for there to be music whose function is to get you high; that's the sort of thing we're hammering at. To get really high is to forget yourself; and to forget yourself is to see everything else; and to see everything else is to become an understanding molecule in evolution, a conscious tool of the universe. That's why I think it's important to get high."

Jerry Garcia, The Grateful Dead.

"I'm for legalizing marijuana. Why pick on those drugs? Valium is legal. You just go to a doctor and get it and overdose on it – what's the difference? Prozac, all that stuff, so why not marijuana? Who cares? It's something that grows out of the ground – why not? Go smoke a head of cabbage. I don't care what you smoke."

Howard Stern, US Radio DJ.

Above: Scenes from a Canadian cannabis celebration, Hempfest in Ontario. Events include music, awards and lots and lots of smoking.

complaining? However, Ramsahai's successes have led him to start up an off shoot Highlife fair and award in Barcelona, Spain, which has already proved successful.

Another Dutch event is Legalize! – an annual street rave also held in Amsterdam, to protest against the war on drugs. It's held on the first weekend of June and isn't just about the legalization of marijuana, but all drugs, hard and soft. The organizers also set up other activities and events against the drug war.

A pleasure doing CannaBusiness

The international CannaBusiness takes place over three days in September. Originally launched in 1996, the show has moved around German venues including Hennef in 1998. The region has a long 'hemp history' which is still alive in the names of the surrounding villages.

But the CannaBusiness fair is never one to rest on its laurels and it currently resides at The Palladium in Cologne, having moved there in 2004. The city is home to the International Association for Cannabis as Medicine (IACM), the Hemp Demo Cologne (www.hanfdemo.de) and *Grow!* Magazine, so it was a very logical move!

The first day used to be reserved for trade visitors, but all three days were opened out to the public by popular demand. 2004 saw a special exhibition of 'Szene Comix' with American creator of The Fabulous Furry Freak Brothers, Gilbert Shelton, along with German artists,

Gerhard Seyfried, Bringmann & Kopetzki, and Steve Stoned, who signed their work for fans. Plus, there was the book launch of *The King of Nepal.* Written by former international cannabis smuggler Joseph Pietri, the book recounts his smuggling days in the Himalayas. The weekend was opened in 2003 with a speech by Werner Sack, a magistrate in Frankfurt's juvenile courts, proving that, while not liberal, Germany's legal system is at least progressive.

Swiss sensi show

Across Europe, other fairs hawk their hempwares. Cannatrade, in Bern, Switzerland, was a relative

Right: Cannabis fairs are perfect places to peruse and purchase all things hempy and to catch up on the latest in growing technologies.

late comer, starting in 2001. Like so many, it began as a small hemp fair and has grown to become a, "reference for the entire hemp market," and a very busy show. The event's aim, to create, "an international hemp network," is coming to fruition, with 164 exhibitors from 15 countries drawing 14,000 visitors - including 900 who were there solely to do business. Cannatrade maintains its roots in cannabis activism, keeping 11 stands available for international hemp associations free of charge, and aims to create a family like, relaxed atmosphere.

Along with all the usual stands - divided into different sections such as Grow It!, Media, Paraphernalia, Institutes, Natural Resources, and Art - there are joint rolling competitions, Swiss hemp initiatives, three fashion shows a day and a spectacular indoor hemp field.

Wandering around the fair are all kinds of colourful characters, such as European cannabis trade show regular Napoleon (dressed as, well, you can guess…) touting his electric weed clipper. Other exhibitors and attendees include the squeaky clean, nay sterile, plant cloners such as Klan Tech, and their antithesis, cannabis shaman, Eagle Bill, who travels around Europe vaporizing people. He was stopped and checked by Belgian police on his way to the 2002 Cannatrade fair, stripped of most of his weed and presented with a 'hefty' 15 Euros fine (£10/$18) that most American smokers would be pleased to get, instead of two years in prison!

"Try before you buy" is the ethos of most cannabis trade fairs, and many a salesman is happy to stuff a bong or vaporizer full of weed so you can see if the product is up to scratch. One such device is the ultimate portable vaporizer – the Vapir. With a digital display and small enough to pocket in an instant, this is the medicinal and pleasure tool of the future. If you want to grow the herb, all the latest gadgets are usually available, from plug and grow kits that do it all for you, to special units that look like fridges to cure your ripe bud.

You might bump into famous authors and medical researchers such as Jos Nijsten, author of *Cannaclopedia*, or attend a seminar by the likes of Dr Ethan Russo, author of *The Official Journal of Cannabis Medicine*, who gave an outstanding presentation in 2002, showing pictures of his growth operations with the UK's GW Pharmaceuticals (see the *Medical marijuana* chapter).

London lights up

London finally woke up to the wonderful world of weed with the first London Hemp Fair in October 2004 at the Wembley Exhibition Centre. It was organised by *Weed World* along with Feria Del Canamo, the organisers of Spannabis, a small fair held in Barcelona in February. The London event was touted by the organizers as, "A lifestyle event where you can meet like

Right: There's nothing finer than toking in the park within the freedom of a festival.

Smoking with Style

A guide to marijuana etiquette

If you want to smoke in polite society, here are some doobie do's and doobie don'ts to make sure you're not excluded the next time a spliff goes round.

1. The person who rolls the joint, lights the joint

There are exceptions to this rule. You may ask someone to roll a joint for you, but they still get to light it unless they specifically tell you to spark it up.

2. Compliment the roller

If someone has built a fantastic joint, compliment them on their rolling skills. You can't bitch about a badly rolled spliff unless you could do better – even then, offer advice rather than bitch; no one needs to feel ragged on when they're getting high.

3. Offer to help

Even the most experienced toker may mess up a roll (there are a lot of factors to take into account – especially after you've smoked a few). Experienced rollers should know how to fix it; if you are dealing with a newbie however, you may want to offer some help with the final touches if you see it all going wrong. Hand it back for them to light though. And get them to practice with just tobacco until they're up to speed.

4. Be quick!

If you are about to put one together, don't get out your stuff and take 20 minutes to roll up.

People will start to get edgy and you'll get a reputation for being a slow roller. Aim to get your time down to under a minute, and be consistent.

5. Don't Bogart

'To Bogart' means to hold on to a spliff for too long without taking a hit and passing it on. It also counts if you are continually lighting it but not taking a toke – that's good weed you're wasting, and your fellow tokers will appreciate it being passed on. The term refers to Humphrey Bogart, who could often be seen with a fag hanging out of his mouth, but very seldom took a drag.

Above: Don't Bogart that joint, Grandad! Take two puffs and pass.

6. Wake the dead

It is good manners to wake someone up when a spliff goes round. If gently saying their name doesn't stir them, then you can carry on passing it round without them taking a hit.

7. Two timing

It is quite common when a lot of spliffs are being passed around, for you to end up with two at the same time. Instead of taking a drag from each one in turn, while everyone else waits, pass one on.

8. Which side?
Musical Youth would have you pass the spliff on the left hand side. Aristocracy would also like to see a bifta passed around to the left (it makes it easier to take with the right hand and, after all, the Port bottle is always passed round to the left), but in this day and age does it really matter? The most important thing is to pass it on!

9. Don't be greedy
If you are in regular company, you will have some idea of how long you can hold on to a joint before your mates start shooting you odd looks. In new company, observe the ritual of the others and follow accordingly. Or simply follow the classic lyrics, "Take two pulls and pass."

10. Don't dribble
There's nothing worse than a spliff with a sodden end, so make sure your lips are dry before taking a toke, and don't dribble on the end. Dribblers rarely get asked back. If you do dribble by mistake, apologise profusely to show that you know you've done wrong.

11. Don't roll for yourself
Some people strategically roll spliffs so that all the good stuff is at the front end. The roller gets all the good hits, and everyone else gets baccy. This is just capitalism in its worst form! Don't do it – your fellow smokers aren't stupid and you'll be quickly ostracized.

12. Bongs, bowls and pipes
Much of the above applies to other smoking devices. Make sure everyone who wants one gets a hit, don't hog it – and roller's rights still apply, "He who stuffs the bowl, lights the bowl."

13. When the stash is low
At those dreaded times when there's little weed or hash left, establish some ground rules before rolling. For instance, if there's only enough left for one spliff, you may want to implement the 'toke 'n' hold' rule – everyone takes one toke and holds the smoke down until it comes their way again. This should make the effect last longer and the weed go further.

14. Repay the favour
If someone has got you stoned in the past, it is good manners to get him or her stoned at some future occasion.

15. Share and share alike
When you've got company, marijuana is for sharing. It is a social drug and your mates will thank you for whipping out a bag of green at a gathering. Although in times of drought it is tempting to hold on to your gear, remember everyone is in the same boat and one day may be able to help you out with a smoke when you need one.

Right: When smoking a joint don't forget your manners; share the weed.

minded people from all over the planet who all have something in common; a love of the herb cannabis, be it sativa, indica or ruderalis."

Like many fairs, London had all of the best cannabis products on 160 stalls, selling everything from hydroponics, hemp clothing and fashion, to pipes, nutrients, digital scales, filter tips, and Hemp Valley Beer. Not forgetting the endless hookahs, magazines, bongs, pollinators, lighting, seeds, organic growing shop, hemp foods and bodycare products on offer. "Everything you could ever want and more," enthused one punter, known as 'Jah Soldier' who, "…could've spent a fortune."

Over the three days, there were talks by Jorge Cervantes (author of the growers' bible, *Indoor Marijuana Horticulture*); international pressure group European Coalition for Just and Effective Drug Policies, on how European drug policy isn't working; and THC4MS who explained how their campaigning for medicinal marijuana has helped ease so many people's suffering in the UK.

There was also a hemp fashion show, revealing designers' latest elegant, modern and tempting creations.

At first there was a reticence to light up, and nobody seemed to be toking in the open. But little obvious police presence soon ensured there was, "Sweet weed scent in the air… everywhere." throughout the weekend.

Unfortunately, the first event had a disappointing turnout due to limited advertising, and verdicts were mixed from, "All huff and no puff" to, "Roll up, roll up, the carnival has come to town!" However, with a change of venue, and a bigger advertising campaign, the fair can only go from strength to Super Skunk strength.

Hippy hemp heaven

Slightly further afield, in the land down under, Aussies are just as passionate about pot. In 1973, university students held the Aquarius Festival in and around the village of Nimbin, an Australian country town on the verge of closing down. Most of the shops were shut so the hippies bought many of the buildings for a song and stayed after the successful festival, Australia's equivalent of Woodstock.

As it grew, Nimbin became a Mecca for those looking for a way of life with values that made sense. Just like Christiana in Denmark, this Australian hippie haven quickly evolved and became self governing. Today, tourists and local people alike have a colourful and dynamic reminder of the origins of counterculture and the plethora of other socio-political issues that have evolved as a result of the increase in awareness. Nimbin is booming. So many who visit and stay a few days want to live there. Perhaps it's the same power and energy the area had for the Aborigines or perhaps it's the hippie values which seem to be making it such a successful community.

Right: Dutch dames dole out dope in Amsterdam's Vondelpark.

Above: Nimbin's MardiGrass is home to the Hemp Olympics and the MMA.

In Nimbin is the Hemp Embassy, which is the historical site for drug law reform activism in Australia, and is the MardiGrass headquarters. The MardiGrass is one of the best organized and most peaceful festivals in Australia and is usually held around the end of April. It has become a respected forum for seminars on industrial hemp, medicinal cannabis, and drug law reform, and is a major boost to the local economy as it attracts Australian and international tourists.

Started in 1992, the MardiGrass bears testimony to the many good people who risk prosecution in the interest of public education and harm minimization. Many are locked up and can't make the festival, and so a minute's silence and the lighting of the flame for victims of prohibition happens at the opening ceremony, at sunset on the Friday.

A kombi konvoy leaves that other Aussie 'alternative' alcove, Byron Bay, on the Saturday and arrives in Nimbin at the classic smoking time, 4.20am, for the attempt at the world record for simultaneous joint lighting.

There are a number of panel discussions and talks on industrial, medicinal, social and political aspects of cannabis use, and visitors are invited to contribute their thoughts on the 'war on drugs' and how it affects their lives. "The thing that makes it special is the enormous number of people who come with good hearts, not only to have a good time, but to show the world just how peaceful, well behaved, organized, creative and talented pot users can be…" the organizers enthused.

The estimated value of Australia's cannabis trade is AUS$8 billion (£3.2 billion/ US$6.1 billion) per year, and a lot of it is smoked by people living in and around Nimbin. "Increasingly, I feel for the police," said Michael Balderstone from the Hemp Embassy, "They don't make the rules, but they have to enforce them… and have no opinion about them, publicly at least! Nimbin is impossible for them. It's in the culture living here now.

"Nimbin's annual rally for help and commonsense is [about] community responses to problems, so we can manage our own affairs more," Balderstone continued. "Let us, and if

Right: If you go down in the woods today, you'll be sure of a big surprise... The Pot Pixies' picnic at Nimbin.

need be - to counter the honey pot effect - a couple of other outlets on the north coast, trial a regulated supply of small amounts of cannabis."

Nimbin locals give their time to help organize the festival, but so do many backpackers, who work in order to get a free weekend pass, which would otherwise cost AUS$20 (£8/US$15).

Understandably, as Australia's drug laws aren't as liberal as Holland's, the Cannabis Cup is held in a secret location each year with judges pulled from a lottery. Also, over the weekend, the Marijuana Music Awards are given out. Launched in 2004, there are two main awards, Best Recorded Track and Best Live Act, with 103 entries from five countries. The awards are open to anyone producing music with a marijuana theme, and past winners have included the bluesy *Rolling Hills Of Nimbin* by Herb Superb, and *Tetra* by Doug Johnson.

The highlight of the MardiGrass is the Rally for Cannabis Law Reform on the Sunday afternoon, when the MardiGrass even holds it's own Hemp Olympix with teams from all over the world. Events include Speed and Blindfolded Joint Rolling, the Bong Throw, and the Grower's Ironperson Event.

There's a major industrial hemp display, with paper making, spinning and weaving fibre, and

Above: An entrepreneur rents out roach clips – hung on his belt, each with a bell! – at the World Music Festival in Los Angeles in 1979.

hemp brick making demonstrations. A Grower's Forum and an Indoor Grow Expo all help share the knowledge, made extremely difficult by prohibition and decades of propaganda. "And of course, all cannabis users should be allowed to grow their own personal stash. This is what MardiGrass is about," said Balderstone.

It all sounds too good to be true!

The Hash Bash

While Nimbin sounds like a smoker's paradise, America is a little harsher on the herb. But, despite desperately outmoded and draconian laws, the spirit of the Sixties still lives on, in the shape of many cannabis festivals all over the country.

The Hash Bash in Ann Arbor, Michigan, is one the longest running annual pot parties in the world. For over 33 years, crowds have gathered in April at the University of Michigan to celebrate cannabis culture and smoke themselves silly. The event has been held every year with the exception of the Reagan era 'Drug War' years (1984-87).

The Ann Arbor Hash Bash started in 1972 as a way to celebrate the change in Michigan's pot law from a felony to a misdemeanour. The spirit of marijuana tolerance was strong in Michigan at the time. Amazingly, liberal State Legislator Perry Bullard even showed up in 1973 to smoke a joint and make a speech at the second festival.

Elsewhere in Michigan State, possession of less than 25 grams of pot is a felony and carries a maximum penalty of a $2,000 fine and/or one year in prison. There is also the lesser offence of

"Use of marijuana" which carries a maximum term of 90 days and/or a $100 fine for anyone who looks stoned!

But the more progressive Ann Arbor voters changed the City Charter to set the fine for marijuana possession at $5. It stayed that way until 1990, when they voted to raise it to $25.

It's safer to smoke on the streets as they're city property, and therefore the only danger is a $25 ticket, though the cops don't usually bother. However, don't smoke pot on the University of Michigan grounds as they're considered State property and the fine, as outlined above, is much heavier. Which is ironic, considering, historically, universities have always been the hotbed of cannabis activity in America since the Sixties.

At its peak, in 1999, the Hash Bash saw regular festival attendees and cannabis celebrities Tommy Chong, Jack Herer and *High Times* editorial alumni Steve Hagar appear. But that same year, the Michigan Senate attempted to introduce a bill prohibiting local authorities from having more lenient marijuana laws than the State, with the specific aim of shutting down the Hash Bash. Despite the cops and the hassle, 5,000 people got together that year to celebrate cannabis culture and have a great time.

But by 2004, attendances had dropped drastically to a mere 650 (according to the Department of Public Safety), partly due to legislation designed to kill the event, including permits not being issued to stall holders in 2002. Regardless of Big Brother's endless attempts to

shut the event down though, Hash Bash still manages to keep going, and the Monroe Street Fair continues to host live bands and musicians such as John Sinclair and his group Glowb, The Process, Troubleman, Rootstand, Mary Eyez and others.

The Hash Bash is organized by the University chapter of the National Organization for the Reform of Marijuana Laws (NORML), and spokesman Josh Soper hopes to increase attendance in order to educate people about marijuana reforms. So get down there and help swell those numbers! Remember, use it or lose it!

USA OK

Apart from the Hash Bash, there's the big Seattle Hempfest in August, and other festivals in Oly (August), Missoula, Montana (September), Ohio (July), and Eugene, Oregon (July), which makes a pretty good tour of the United Stoners of America. All of these fairs have been going for at least eight years, but many still operate on a shoestring budget in a constant battle with belligerent bureaucracy – the Eugene hempfest had to be cancelled in 2004 because of such problems.

The Johnes (pronounced 'Johns') Festival is a typically skint event. It's an Earth Day festival for marijuana reform, sponsored by Western Connecticut State University chapter NORML (now known as WCSU NORML). It was founded as a result of a vision of Chad Westerberg from Waterbury, CT in early 1996. He approached

Personal Highs:
Californian sunshine

In 1979, Cal Morgan (AKA Cynthia Morgan) and her fellow Californian hippie grass growers vowed to live in peaceful fellowship and never cultivate just for the sake of making money. Five years of herbal horticulture saw those ideals collapse like a house of cards when she ended up poaching from poachers, lying to liars, and swindling swindlers.

Knives, guns, threats, broken contracts, rattlesnakes and rats all played a part in the tumultuous tree hugger's cannabis cultivating career. She formed several nefarious partnerships with an aikido teacher, a former prostitute, an ex-49er American football player, an embezzler, and an airplane pilot. Each successive season saw her planting more and more marijuana as she dug herself deeper into trouble.

Finally, it all came to a head in 1984 when, returning to her secluded California farmhouse, she heard the words any grower fears.

"'Stop the truck and put both hands out the window!' Who said that? I slam my foot on the brakes and look in the rear view mirror. What in the... Where did those four men holding guns come from? And why are their guns pointed at me? 'Put both hands out the window!' I turn off the engine and hurl my right hand out the window. One of the men breaks away from the group and scuttles crab like towards me. My God, he's acting the way cops do when they're moving in on a criminal. 'Get out of the truck with your hands up!' Shit! I'm getting busted!"

The cops took her up to the house where, "The cop across the table reaches into his back pocket, takes out his wallet, flips it open with his thumb and pulls forth a faded card. 'You have the right to remain silent...' Frantically, I search my mind. What do I have in the house that's illegal? Let's see... There's that baggy of seeds in the drawer under the elbow of the guy holding the grocery bag... Those photographs Will took last year, of me holding a couple of twelve foot plants in Bonny Doon... Oh no! The scales in the linen closet!"

But Morgan couldn't understand what was going on, as she'd been busted before, "This is not the way it was supposed to happen. After they pulled the plants you were supposed to invite them inside for a cup of coffee. After drinking the coffee they were supposed to tell you, 'It's too bad we have these laws but they'll change soon. Thanks for the coffee.' Then they were supposed to leave without arresting you.

"Oh no! The scales in the linen closet!"

"The refrigerator inspector is standing in front of the bookcase. All the books he's been rifling through are scattered around the floor at his feet. In his hands are the photos I hid in a gardening book. He's staring at the one Will took of me holding a giant sensimilla, its branches cascading over my bare breasts. He shows the photo to Barker. The grocery bag scrutinizer joins them. The doorway guard comes out from the bedroom carrying Will's gun and soon they're passing around the photographs..."

Morgan was eventually busted by the Santa Cruz County Sheriff's Department for growing half a million dollars worth of marijuana. She sat on the story for many years thinking about how to present it, and eventually wrote the autobiographical *10 Foolish Fortune Hunters*, a tale much greater than the sum of its many daring escapades and the individuals who played their part, that was published in 2000. Morgan has since forgone cannabis cultivating and has taken up the safer hobby of quilting. Whether she uses hemp cloth is unknown.

Above: You want it? I got it! A portable head shop in a box at a cannabis festival.

NORML with the idea and the inaugural event was held in 1998. The annual festival takes place in April at the Charles Ives Center for the Arts on Western Connecticut State University's Westside Campus.

Diverse speakers in the past have included revolutionary rabble rouser Rob Krause, Sylvester Lee Salcedo – a retired naval intelligence officer – and Clifford Thornton, President of Efficacy, a non-profit drug reform organization.

The Jacksonville Hempfest takes place around May or June at the Seawalk Pavilion in Jacksonville Beach, Florida. The one day event started in 1997 with the aim of educating the public about hemp and its many industrial uses, about medical cannabis, and about the many, many people arrested on trumped up cannabis charges in the USA. Past speakers included Loretta Nall, the President of the US Marijuana Party, and Alex White Plume, a Lakota-Oglala Indian, whose industrial hemp crops were destroyed by federal agents, because they can't tell the difference between grass that'll get you high and grass that's just good for making clothes.

Hemp hemp hooray

While the American government may be 'The Great Beast', Canada's cannabis policies are ever so slightly less damaging. As recently as 2002, the Senate Special Committee on Illegal Drugs announced, "The continued prohibition of cannabis jeopardizes the health and well being of Canadians much more than does the substance

Above: Festival friends in a field smoke a bowl or two.

Left: Canabian Day is just one of many Canadian cannabis festivals held each year.

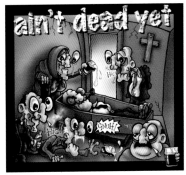

Right: The American alternative music festival, Ain't Dead Yet, is "hemp friendly".

itself." Consequently, there are many cannabis festivals across the country that have more latitude than their southern neighbours.

The second Canabian Day Festival held in 2004 simultancously in Toronto, Hamilton and Niagara, went off without a hitch with demonstrators treating, with respect, the event location and the police who, in turn, allowed the organizers the freedom to gather and demonstrate without interference. Such gatherings are becoming increasingly common in Canada as the cannabis legalization movement continues to strengthen. The country is closer to legalization now than it has been since the Le Dain Commission in 1973 (when all its members supported the decriminalization of cannabis). And probably closer than America would like, as it tries to maintain a discrediting propaganda war against the Canuck nation.

However, the really big Canadian event is the Hempfest near Sault Ste Marie. Once a year – deep in Canada's scenic northern Ontario forests – a population the size of a small town gathers to celebrate the cannabis plant.

The four day event includes over 12 bands, fire dancers, vendors, speakers, exhibits, a laser light show, and most of all, the finest cannabis from around the world. Hempfest operates on a similar basis as the infamous Burning Man Festival in Nevada, since both act as temporary communities.

Left: The Burning Man Festival brings new meaning to the phrase, "Altered States".

Nothing is bought or sold at Hempfest, apart from a few things such as food and drink, toothpaste and a few memorabilia and gifts to take back home. There's also a Dutch style 'coffee shop', selling everyone's favourite herb. The whole event is self policed and hasn't had any altercations or incidents in five years. It also shows that the organizers can handle 1,100 Hempfest citizens with the respect and tact that the police sometimes forget. At past festivals, speakers such as Grant Krieger, Rick Reimer, Rob Waddell and Robert Neron – Canada's premier medicinal marijuana smoker, grower and activist – have kept audiences enraptured.

Features include a techno stage, "Le Club Chronique", a main stage for live acts, and a donation bar opening at 2.30am. 2005 even saw the introduction of the Naked Hippie Mud Slide competition! During the day, contests include the scrap metal Bong Wars with two categories, Best of Show and a Modified Category. In 2004, the Treatingyourself.com crew won hands down with their Junk Yard Bong, and a Modified Electric Gas Mask took the Modified Category. The Rolling Contest was reclaimed by Robert Neron for his marijuana leaf joint. The GMC Crew took the Big Bud Weigh In, with a stunning 47.6 gram bud in 2003, a record yet to be beaten. All Big Bud entries are shared with the crowd and they went wild trying to get a piece of the action. And the newest event is the Half Gram Sprint, to see who can smoke their stash the fastest. 2004's winner asked to remain anonymous, possibly because he couldn't remember his own name after such an intense hit! Also during the excitement, $\pm 1/4$ pound of high quality pot, 5,000 seeds from Robert Neron and all kinds of papers, pipes and swag were given away.

But things don't always go so smoothly for every celebration. 2004's marijuana friendly Freedomfest was 'postponed' for reasons unclear. The three day music festival posted on their web site the enigmatic, "Freedomfest has always stood up for your rights, believe it or not, you do have some! Freedomfest continues to fight for them for you. We hope to have your support. FREEDOMFEST WILL HAPPEN! Freedomfest will not be cancelled by the MAN or anyone else under any circumstances! Freedomfest will honour your tickets." However, by mid-2005 the postponement notice on the site was still up. Whether the MAN had got to them remains unknown at this stage.

The ultimate pot party

But if you prefer your sensimilla celebrations somewhere sunnier, you couldn't have done better than Psytopia. The seven day psychedelic convention was the ultimate in luxury festivals, held in August 2005 at Hedonism III in Jamaica.

Arranged by Alex Pearlstein, President of Tripatourium – a publisher of limited edition blotter art – the event was designed as a fundraiser for five drug reform charities; MAPS, NORML, The Albert Hofmann Foundation, the Chapel of Sacred Mirrors, and The Drug Policy Alliance. Pearlstein's choice of NORML is not surprising as he sits on the Board of Directors for the Massachusetts chapter. The idea for Psytopia was, "One big party where all of humanity comes together and becomes interconnected. Where not only are all invited but all attend and, in doing so, there is no more 'them' but a unified 'us'," explained Pearlstein.

Psytopia took over both Hedonism III and Breezes Runaway Bay, and only attendees of the event were allowed in for seven days of luxury. The one price, pot package holiday covered all food and drinks, 14 bands, 21 speakers, 14 DJs, nightly concerts on the beach, laser shows, circus schools, SCUBA diving, sailing, snorkeling and surprises. Speakers included the artist Alex Grey, and members of MAPS, NORML, *High Times* and The Church of the Subgenius. Even high profile bands like My Life, Thrill Kill Kult and Ozric Tentacles played.

This was as far away as you could get from the quaint days of a few hippies gathering to listen to a local band in a park, waving a few placards and smoking a few spliffs. It seems that the age of the super festival is here. Whether they turn out to be all inclusive, as cannabis events have traditionally been, or simply for a few, rich elite intellectuals who want to get stoned on a beach without the 'riff raff', remains to be seen.

Right: Rollin' one for the road on the Glastonbury trail, where the grass grows free.

Chapter 6

Cannabis lifestyle

Cannabis is all around us. Cannabis ruderalis, 'industrial hemp', that is. It can be found in the food we eat, the clothes we wear and the things we use. In fact, it's incredibly easy to lead the complete, sustainable hemp lifestyle, as this extract from Harry the Happy Hempster's diary shows.

Cannabis Lifestyle

I wake up at ten, pull back my soft, 100% hemp blankets, crawl out of bed and head for the bathroom. Climbing into the shower, I pull the hemp curtain behind me (www.ahappyplanet.com). The curtain is made from extremely strong and durable Romanian hemp fabric. It stops water splashing and, with only a plastic liner, helps keep unnatural plastics out of our landfills. It also air dries rapidly, preventing mould growth associated with plastic curtains.

Right: No one can call you a smelly hippy with the all the hemp toiletries available.

I wash myself with Dr Bonner's famous 18-in-1 Hemp Almond organic soap (www.drbronner.com) and a hemp flannel. Then I wash my hair with Yaoh's Organic Hemp Seed Oil Shampoo and Conditioner (www.yaoh.co.uk). They are free from harmful, and unnecessary, chemical additives, so my lovely locks don't fall out!

Drying myself down with a hemp towel, I then get dressed, putting on super comfortable socks

Above: The ultra cool Ipath skate shoes are made from tough hemp.

and boxer shorts. Hemp is great for underwear as it has naturally occurring anti-fungal and anti-bacterial properties, and is great for drawing moisture away from the skin, so no smelly feet or painful crotch itch! Then it's on with my trousers. If I'm feeling particularly 'hempy', I'll forego the vintage Levi's jeans (which include 40% hemp) and go the whole hog with a pair of hemp canvas Carpenter pants from Hemp Braintree (www.braintreehemp.com.au).

The trousers are held up with a 100% hemp Banzai Belt from www.hempest.com and topped off with a politically cool 'Smoke Bush' T-shirt from the funky fashionistas at The Hemp Trading Company (www.thtc.co.uk). Finally, I put on my Yogi Lo Saddle Hemp trainers (www.ipath.com). After some quick hair styling with hemp based Knotty Boy Dread Wax (www.knottyboy.com), I make for the kitchen.

For breakfast I normally eat hemp toast or Hanf & Natur's muesli with German hemp seeds, and drink a fresh cup of real Indian Sativa Hemp Coffee (www.Spiritstream.com) filtered through a 100% hemp coffee filter, of course! Then I check my Hemp Industries Association's (www.thehia.org) hemp calendar (printed on recycled you know what) for any important events in the stoner calendar. Today is actually my girlfriend's birthday, so I put on my hemp baseball cap and hemp jacket, grab my hemp bag and put the hemp collar and lead on my dog Molly, and head for the shops to buy a present.

I love to ride down the road on my Hempcore skateboard (www.hempcore.com) as Molly pulls me along. Compared to the majority of maple wood decks, boards incorporating hemp are 20% stronger and last longer. And they save maple trees!

At the shops I buy a birthday card and envelope (both printed on hemp paper) and

Right: It's possible to kit your entire wardrobe out solely with hemp wear.

A history of
High Times

Few marijuana magazines have survived for very long, with publishers either losing interest or governmental forces shutting them down. But 2004 saw the 30th anniversary of the US magazine *High Times*, renowned around the world for its in depth articles about anything to do with grass, for setting up and running the yearly Cannabis Cup and, of course, centrefolds of sticky ganja made to make your mouth water. The continued use of a centrefold is a reminder of *High Times'* origins when, back in 1974, the magazine was intended as a one-off lampoon of *Playboy*, substituting smoking buds for smoking bods.

Those early issues were put together and published by Thomas King Forcade, an underground journalist, anti-war activist, concert promoter and publisher. However, it was his other income as a high flying dope smuggler that provided the funds to get the magazine off the ground. Its initial focus was not just on Mary Jane, but also her more psychedelic friends; 'shrooms and LSD. Even cocaine got a look in during the early days. The staff were counterculture rebels who knew people were getting high and wanted to read about and experiment with the drugs available to them. Although it may sound like the ideal gonzo-journalistic gig, working for Forcade was a wild ride, and he was well known for pitting staff against one another. Possibly a touch of post-smoke paranoia hit Forcade one afternoon when he decided to sack all the staff, but he'd obviously come down by the next day, inviting them back to work again.

Tragically, Forcade committed suicide in 1978, but by then he had seen the ostensibly underground magazine reach a circulation of over 420,000. He left it in the hands of friend and lawyer Michael Kennedy, whose knowledge of the drugs scene was considerable – he had represented LSD visionary Timothy Leary and members of his followers, Weather Underground, in court trials. Around this time, the magazine's focus shifted to mainly marijuana, becoming a one stop publication for the stoner, supporting and starting huge events like a Bob Marley

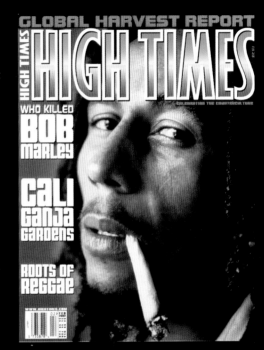

Above: High Times covers serious sensimellia journalism, such this article on Bob Marley.

festival in Miami, and the annual Cannabis Cup in Amsterdam, now in its 18th year. The Cup started when the now Editor in Chief of *High Times*, Steven Hager, was researching an article in the Netherlands in 1987. He was there to interview the so called King Of Cannabis (an Australian called Nevil), who reportedly lived in a mansion filled with growing rooms, after a mail order cannabis company he started made him rich. As part of the feature, Hager met owners of an almost defunct American seed company call Cultivators Choice. They regaled him with tales of the California harvest festivals in the Seventies, and the idea for an international festival was born.

So how does a magazine that celebrates the smoking and growing of pot survive in the USA, where the current government (and those before it) are officially at war with drugs? As Editor Steve Bloom explained to *The Boston Phoenix*, America's first amendment (Freedom of Speech) keeps the government away, "That's how we can publish this magazine about an illegal subject without being censored, without being harassed." The photo shoots are another matter though, "The large variety of stuff you see in the magazine is technically illegal. If the government wants to look into that, I suppose they would. I hope they don't. I hope they have better things to worry about than where the pot is coming from for a *High Times* photo shoot."

However, for most of its life, *High Times* has managed to stay out of trouble although it has been hit hard by being indirectly involved in a couple of busts. One such bust, Operation Green Merchant in May 1991, attempted to shut down indoor growing activities in the US by targeting both the growers and those companies that supplied the various tools of the trade. According to reports, the DEA used the magazine to get to the companies by looking at the various adverts and putting two and two together. Even more recently, Operation Pipe Dreams, which focused on sellers of bongs, bowls and pipes and saw famous dope star Tommy Chong sent to prison, cost *High Times* dearly in advertising, and the magazine's once healthy readership took a dip to below 100,000. It coincided with a management feeling that *High Times* had become old and tired, so the whole mag was revamped – the marijuana being mostly replaced by stories on lifestyle and other related issues. So absent was the mighty weed that a quarterly supplement was also published to give tokers the latest news on weed related matters. This re-launch was an unmitigated disaster and the magazine was finally given back to some old timer staff who reintroduced everything that had made it great and, surprise surprise, the circulation has started to creep back up.

It continues to promote the bud like before and, with an ever growing source of A-list stars (including the likes of Tenacious D's Jack Black and Kyle Gass, Ozzy Osbourne, Marilyn Manson, Snoop Dogg, Ice Cube, Ali G, and Method Man) willing to be seen on the cover and to speak out about the ludicrous laws regarding the plant, it looks like the next generation of heads will see it through tough times in the US and around the world, where cannabis is still considered to be a harmful drug.

SUPER 420 ISSUE

HIGH TIMES

CELEBRATING THE COUNTERCULTURE

FRANCES
McDORMAND
HOLLYWOOD
SUPERSTAR

THE BEST
STONER
GEAR

PURPLE
POT

IN SEARCH OF
MAJOR
NUGGS

HIGH TIMES

SOLUTIONS FOR SICK GARDENS

STAIND
GET STOND

TOP-RATED
SEEDS
FROM HOLLAND

WOMEN
OF GLASS

THE CIA
& THE TALIBAN

SHOOTOUT
AT RAINBOW
FARM

STAIND STONER
AARON
LEWIS

HIGH TIMES

CELEBRATING THE COUNTERCULTURE

POT STRAINS OF THE FUTURE

GEAR
OF THE
YEAR
5TH STASH
AWARDS

FAMILY
GROW
TEAM

FEDS
BUST
BONGS

65 | 121 | 68

WWW.HIGHTIMES.COM

Covers: Despite its tumultuous and fractious history, High Times magazine has become a stoner institution and appearing on the cover ensures instant street cred for stars such as Fargo actress, Frances McDormand.

manage to get a Cowry Shell Tribal Hemp Choker (also available at www.hempjewelryshop.com). Next I pick up a pro-pot chill out CD, 'Fields of Green', featuring a 100% hemp didgeridoo. Amazingly, the case is the first ever commercial hemp plastic product, thanks to the whizzes at www.hempplastic.com. This biodegradable hemp plastic CD tray is helping the environment by creating an alternative to petro-chemicals. As I pull out my black Romanian hemp wallet (www.ahappyplanet.com) to pay, I'm reminded that over 600,000 acres of hemp is grown worldwide, in countries as diverse as Germany and China, and it's helping Romania to rebuild its economy. Yet it's still illegal to grow industrial hemp in America, despite the fact that you can't get stoned on it. Weird.

For lunch, I have a salad drizzled with cold pressed hemp seed oil from China. This is the best way to eat it, because if the oil is overheated, the health benefits of the essential fatty acids can be lost. In some cases, it can even turn the oil carcinogenic. The oil gives the salad a slightly nutty flavour, plus, I sprinkle a few de-hulled hemp seeds on it. For pudding I have a Yaoh Coconut and Pineapple Raw Food

Left: Get the right hemp for the job. Sativa for smoking, Ruderalis for rope making.

Right: Mary Jane eases the pain against laws that are insane.

Above: The design says it all; bedspreads are best when made with buds.

Organic Hemp Snack Bar which won Best Organic Product at the Brighton Natural Products show in 2004. Over lunch, I catch up with my bi-monthly fix of Cannabis Culture magazine. CC is a Vancouver, Canada-based publication about marijuana and hemp around the world. It hasn't lost its sense of humour as it fights to liberate marijuana, free pot-prisoners and bring an end to the war on drugs, while also supplying the best cultivation info and news,

complimented by the most beautiful bud shots. You'll find the best writers and photographers of the industry here! Dana Larsen was the outstanding editor up until issue 55, when publisher Marc Emery took the editorial helm. Over 10 years in print, and it still keeps me surprised and informed. In between issues I catch up on the latest growing tech developments, daily international marijuana-related news coverage, and the ongoing legalization campaigns at www.cannabisculture.com.

Then I head to the park. It's a hot, sunny day so I put on some Hemp Sun Block and play on a different type of grass with Molly; throwing her my hemp frisbee (www.ecolution.com) which she catches in mid-air. On the way home, I fall off my skateboard and scrape my hands.

Back home, I pause outside and marvel at the technical achievement of the house. It was built using materials from Isochanvre SARL, a French company that has helped build over 250 hemp homes, including the ones in Suffolk, England (www.suffolkhousing.org). The walls are made from hemp fibre mixed with lime to create a thermal and acoustic barrier which is as strong as concrete, but seven times lighter. Other parts of the house made from hemp include the fibreboard, panelling, particleboard, plaster, plywood, reinforced concrete flooring and

Right: If you don't wear weed, at least eat it! There are hemp versions of nearly all food.

Coffee shop conflict

Amsterdam: All that art, all those tulips, and all those coffee shops where you can buy cannabis with your cappuccino or marijuana with your mocha. Could this ever happen in the UK or US?

In 2004, the UK took a big step towards realigning its feelings about cannabis by downgrading it from a Class B to a Class C drug. But are we any nearer to the dream of Dutch freedom? Where scoring doesn't mean meeting a friend of a friend down a dark side street, but popping into a coffee shop and ordering a drink and nice little bag of whatever you fancy?

In a word, no. The government's new stance on the drug has not made it any more legal to buy and sell; you just stand much less chance of being arrested for private use. However, those choosing to sell large amounts or keep a stock on premises, like cafés, are open to all sorts of prosecutions that don't really take into account the classification of cannabis.

Amsterdam coffee shops also face similar problems (they can't sell large amounts, or keep a large stock on the premises), but public toleration of such grey areas is grudgingly higher in the Netherlands than in the UK.

But that hasn't stopped people trying to capture the Dutch experience. One publican in Great Yarmouth, Michael Skipper, tried openly selling it in his pub, the Gallery Bar, for a while, but pretty soon his license was revoked and he had to pay £3,000 in court costs. "I intended the bar to be used by artists, but now I'll have to find someone else to run it," complained Skipper. "I was making a political and social statement because cannabis use is rife in Great Yarmouth."

London's Green Leaf Café (jerk chicken out front, primo bud out back) was shut down and its owner jailed for six and a half years. In Dorset however, Jimmy Ward walked free from court after being arrested for running a cannabis café, when he pointed out that his premises had plenty of signage stating that smoking cannabis was not permitted. A trick he perhaps learned

Right: The Purple Haze café in Leith, Scotland was the focus of pro-legalization.

in a BBC documentary he took part in, in which he attended a course in the Netherlands on how to run a Dutch-style coffee shop! Ward's lawyer astutely pointed out, "He [Ward] wanted to be ready for the legalization of the drug so he could be a front runner in the cannabis movement, but in doing so he put himself at risk of going further than the law… His intention was to set up an information and advice centre, not a cannabis cafe."

Even in Scotland, openly selling the drug will lead to a visit from the police – as Paul Stewart, the owner of the internet café Purple Haze in Glasgow found out, after only several hours of being open. He escaped with a £500 fine, but the stress and disappointment forced him to put the place up for sale.

In the US, things are much worse. Whereas the UK tolerates head shops selling all sorts of drug related paraphernalia, the Feds in the US still bust people on a regular basis for selling pipes, chillums and bongs – including cannabis hero and star of many films, Tommy Chong, whose glass company Chong Glass, was raided in 2004 along with his house. Tommy got nine months in prison – for selling bongs and papers. The chances of being able to sit down and smoke a joint in a café in the US, under the current political climate, is remote to say the least.

Right: Brixton, London became "Little Amsterdam" when local police declared an

Above: Needless to say organic hemp lipstick is not tested on little furry animals.

roofing. The hardened material is resistant to rotting, rodents, insects and fire. The loft is lined with hemp legend Ben Dronkers' Hempflax insulation (www.hempflax.com). Not only does it keep the house warm, but hemp fibre soaks up and distributes moisture, which results in optimal moisture regulation, meaning no nasty condensation. The concrete pipes are reinforced with hemp fibre and cost less than one third of the price of conventional polypropylene reinforced concrete pipes and have greater flexibility and resistance to cracking. Fibreboard made from hemp is twice as strong, and three times more elastic than fibreboard made from wood. Why use 300 year old trees to make a home that will last some 50 years, when you can use 90 day old hemp to build the same house? The answer seems obvious to me.

It suddenly dawns on me that there's virtually nothing this amazing plant can't do! Hemp is the world's most versatile fibre and, to date, there are more than 25,000 known uses for it!

In the kitchen I get some Hemp Oil Salve and put it on my scraped hands. I wrap my girlfriend's birthday presents with hemp paper and string, then start to make a birthday cake with hemp flour from Emerald The Hemp Company of America (www.hempnutts.com).

To set the mood, I light some hemp-soy-palm candles which I bought from www.earthfriendlygoods.com. The candles incorporate hemp seed oil and hemp cored wicks, and with their aromatherapy properties, are great at setting the mood.

My girlfriend, Mary Jane, and our friends turn up in their hemp car. For fuel, it uses hemp biodiesel, which is created from hemp oil and will run in any conventional, unmodified diesel engine. Hemp biodiesel produces about 80% less CO_2 emissions and almost 100% less sulphur dioxide. It is as biodegradable as sugar,

Right: One of today's biggest uses of hemp is for bags, rucksacks and fashionable clothing.

Personal Highs:

Dental dope damage

Getting high can sometimes also mean some pretty painful lows, as cannabis cultural critic and THC Sacrament Minister, Reverend Vern Paiyne (AKA Viper) found out. Viper was in Amsterdam for the 2003 Cannabis Cup. As he reported on his infamous web site, www.viperslair.co.uk, he was in the appropriately named Amnesia coffee shop, toking from a vaporizer.

"I took the hit and I remember thinking, 'Wow, what a great hiiiiiiiiiiiiiit!' Far better than anything I'd smoked so far this trip. This shit could definitely leave Soma's NYC diesel standing. However, I was faintly aware something wasn't quite right. I remember I was still holding the hit in and I slowly released it."

But then it all went a bit Pete Tong.

"It seems that following the hit, I'd sat up briefly then just dropped forwards like a felled tree. My head had collided with the bar hard and loud enough to scare everybody in the coffee shop... They thought I was dead to begin with. I'm told I was out cold for about five seconds. Then the darkness began to dissipate and my vision came back. I saw three concerned faces looking down at me in a cartoon like circle.

"'What happened?' I began, whilst spitting out nasty gritty bits of shit I thought were off the floor, when all of a sudden I was propelled into a world of pain. Somewhere above my left eye felt like it had been hit with something like a piece of 4 x 2 planed finish. There were still bits of something hard & gritty in my mouth so I spat them out. I was still holding the balloon. I let it go. Then I realized what those hard bits might be. Sure enough, my front teeth were broken. I counted five. A little piece fell off as I tentatively tongued the new, jagged ivory landscape... The side of my face was a different matter; I could feel swelling and large scale bruising on the way. The pain was sickening."

Then I realized what those hard bits might be. Sure enough, my front teeth were broken.

But Viper shrugged it off with typical Scouse bravado, "I'm from Liverpool, mate. They make us from hardened stuff back there." When he returned to the Cannabis Cup the following day he, "...was surprised to find all manner of stall holders and helpers came forward during the day to point out their membership of the Stoners' Busted Tooth Club. I was a fully paid up member of the insiders' SBTC now.

"What they all wanted to know was... just what had wiped out this Amsterdam veteran of 13 years' hard toking, this Scouse hero of 17 plus years' smoking experience? The guy who was always last to leave the HH bar at night and first to enter for breakfast next morning. What had brought this Viper down?"

The answer? "Sweet Alaskan from Apothecary Seeds in a Volcano vaporizer."

You have been warned!

Above: Hemp food has all the taste without giving you the munchies.

10 times less toxic than table salt, and has been proven as a successful fuel in over 30 million US road miles, and for over 20 years of use in Europe. Not only that, but the exhaust odour is the pleasant smell of hemp. Henry Ford of course, went one step further in 1941 by building his infamous plastic car out of hemp and wheat straw.

Mary Jane looks fantastic in her black Firenze hemp dress (www.ecolution.com). I serve a selection of hemp beers including Cannabia from Germany, the UK's Greenleaf's Hemp Ale, and Australia's Burke's Hemp Ale (www.hempbeer.com). Hemp is a vegetable cousin to hops, so it makes excellent beer. I also mix a few cannabis cocktails with Austrian hemp vodka, using the recipes from *Spliffs 2*, and pass round Ruth's Chili Lime Hemp Chips (www.ruthshempfoods.com).

For dinner, I serve Hanf & Natur's Organic Hemp Spaghetti with a bolognaise sauce and we toast the birthday girl with Swiss Chanvrin Mousseux hemp champagne (www.sensiseeds.com). Dessert is Mellow Yellow Ice Cream (from a *Spliffs 1* recipe) and HempHog Milk Chocolate Truffles with hemp nut cream filling. Then I bring out the giant, green, seven leafed cake and we sing 'Happy birthday'.

After dinner, we crash into the hemp beanbags (www.beanproducts.com) and sit around listening to Bob Marley blasting out of the hemp speakers. We play Grow Op (www.growopgame.com), the board game based on becoming an herbal horticulturalist and dealer. It was banned by the New York Toy Fair because it violated the Fair's values and mandate, "to support positive development of children" – despite all the war and gun games available at the show. My mate Howard wins the game and I skin up a few celebratory joints of Heaven's Haze.

Above: Of course, if you are going to smoke grass, make sure you use hemp-made rolling papers and roaches.

Right: Be a Merry Hempster and use vegan hemp balm – the hip trip for lips – to protect your chapped lips in winter.

Eventually our friends stagger off, leaving Mary Jane and I alone. She smiles sexily at me as we both slip, semi-stoned, between our hemp sheets. As we kiss, I can taste her cherry flavoured, hemp based lip balm. "Yup, the hemper home is a happy one," I think, as I reach for the hemp oil based Canolio SexyGanja™ Personal Lubricant (www.globalhempstore.com).

Chapter 7

Skins and Things

The humble joint; where would we be without it? Left with a big pile of grass we'd have to set fire to a bonfire, that's where. Yup, thanks to the wonderful invention of rolling papers, you can forget all the paraphernalia like bongs, vaporizers and pipes. All you need to get traditional is some skins, Zags or Rizzies, and a roach to get nicely toasted...

BAMBU BIG HEMP *(left)*

LAUNCHED IN SPAIN IN 1764 BAMBU PAPERS' KEY SELLING POINT WAS ITS ALL NATURAL GUM SEALER MADE FROM THE AFRICAN ACACIA TREE. THE PAPERS WERE A HUGE SUCCESS AT THE BEGINNING OF THE 20TH CENTURY, STARRING IN FILMS, ON THE BACK OF BUSES AND EVENTUALLY ON TELEVISION. UNFORTUNATELY, THE 'WAR ON DRUGS' AND NANCY AND RONALD REAGAN'S 'JUST SAY NO' CAMPAIGN IN THE 1980s BROUGHT AN END TO ROLLING PAPER ADVERTISING. AS IF THE PAPERS COULDN'T BE USED TO SIMPLY ROLL A TOBACCO CIGARETTE! STILL, BAMBU SURVIVED AND WEAR THEIR ECO-FRIENDLY PRIDE ON THEIR PRODUCT WITH THESE HEMP PAPERS.

BIG BAMBU *(right)*

THE BIG BAMBU WAS THE PAPER OF CHOICE FOR AMERICAN STONERS IN THE SEVENTIES. THE BRAND WAS IMMORTALIZED BY CHEECH AND CHONG AS THE NAME OF THEIR CLASSIC 1972 COMEDY ALBUM – CONSIDERED ONE OF THEIR FUNNIEST. THE COVER WAS EVEN DESIGNED TO LOOK LIKE A GIANT PACKET, ENSURING THE ROLLING PAPER'S COOL CANNABIS CONNECTION. TODAY, BAMBU SELL STYLISH CAPS AND FUNKY T-SHIRTS WITH THEIR CLASSIC WINKING SPANIARD LOGO.

GOLDEN WRAP CHOC *(right)*
THESE CHOCOLATE FLAVOURED PAPERS
FROM REPUBLIC TOBACCO MAY JUST MAKE
THE MUNCHIES A BIT EASIER TO HANDLE.
JOINTS CAN BE ROLLED IN PRACTICALLY
ANYTHING, AND PAPERS COME IN A HUGE
VARIETY, FROM FLAVOURED PAPERS LIKE THIS AND
HEMP ONES OPPOSITE, TO THOSE MADE FROM RICE
PAPER, MAIZE PAPER, CORN LEAVES (ALSO KNOWN AS
BRAZILIAN PALHAS) AND AS EVERY HIP HOP HEMPER
KNOWS, BLUNTS MADE FROM TOBACCO LEAVES.

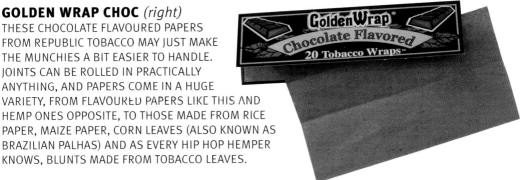

PLAYING CARDS *(left)*
GAMBLING IS A MUG'S GAME BUT
IF YOU PLAY FOR SPLIFFS IT'S A
DIFFERENT MATTER. PLAY YOUR
CARDS RIGHT WITH THIS WEED
INSPIRED HEMP CULTURE DECK.
YOU CAN HAVE FUN AND LEARN
ABOUT THE DUTCH WAY OF DOPE
AT THE SAME TIME.

STASH MAGIC BOX *(left)*

IT'S ALL VERY WELL HAVING A HUGE STASH OF PRIMO GEAR BUT WHAT IF YOUR MATES WANT TO NICK IT ALL? WORSE, THE POLICE DECIDE TO PAY A VISIT. YOU NEED TO HIDE THAT STASH! THE MAGIC BOX IS THE THING FOR YOU. NOT ONLY DOES IT KEEP ALL YOUR PAPERS AND GEAR NEATLY PACKED AWAY, BUT IT'S IMPOSSIBLE TO OPEN WITHOUT KNOWING ABOUT THE SECRET UNLOCKING MECHANISM. SAFE, SECURE AND SWEET!

GOLDEN WRAP COCO *(right)*

IN JULY 1999, ONE OF THE WORLD'S BIGGEST ROLLING PAPER COLLECTORS, TONI SEGARRA, SOLD HIS COLLECTION OF OVER 5,560 PAPERS TO SPANISH ROLLING PAPER MANUFACTURER MIQUEL Y COSTAS & MIQUEL. A CONDITION OF THE SALE WAS THAT THE COLLECTION WAS TO BE AVAILABLE TO THE GENERAL PUBLIC, AND SO IT WAS HOUSED IN THE PAPER MUSEUM IN THE SAME VILLAGE AS MCM'S FACTORY.

JUICY JAY'S (above)
THESE DAYS THERE ARE MANY PEOPLE COLLECTING ROLLING PAPERS, FROM ANTIQUE ONES TO THE LATEST RELEASES. IMPORTANT POINTS COLLECTORS LOOK OUT FOR ARE THE CONDITION, THE AGE, WEIGHT AND WHAT GUM OR OTHER CHEMICALS WERE USED. TO MAKE THINNER PAPER, MORE EMULSION IS USED IN THE PROCESS. A PAPER'S COUNTRY OF ORIGIN IS ANOTHER FACTOR AND IS PARTICULARLY HARD TO CATEGORISE, AS MANY PAPERS HAVE BEEN MADE IN ONE COUNTRY, PACKAGED IN ANOTHER, AND FINALLY DISTRIBUTED AND SOLD IN MANY OTHERS.

JUICY JAY'S BLUE (right)
THESE BEST SELLING FLAVOURED PAPERS ARE NAMED AFTER THE CO-FOUNDER'S NICKNAME RATHER THAN A JOINT. THE MIND BLOWING RANGE OF FLAVOURS INCLUDES MARSHMALLOW, PEACHES & CREAM, ABSINTHE, CANDY HEARTS, TEQUILA AND SIZZLING BACON!

195

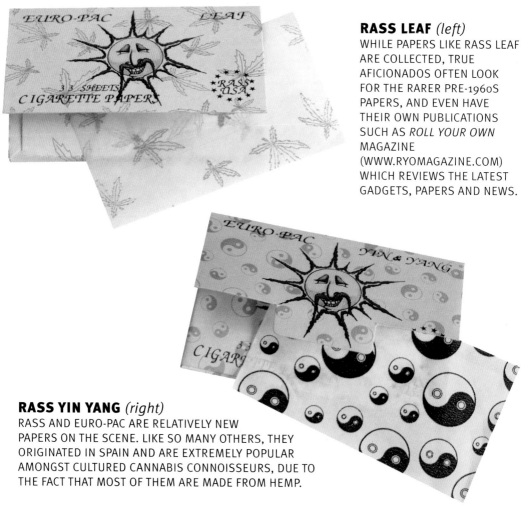

RASS LEAF *(left)*
WHILE PAPERS LIKE RASS LEAF ARE COLLECTED, TRUE AFICIONADOS OFTEN LOOK FOR THE RARER PRE-1960S PAPERS, AND EVEN HAVE THEIR OWN PUBLICATIONS SUCH AS *ROLL YOUR OWN* MAGAZINE (WWW.RYOMAGAZINE.COM) WHICH REVIEWS THE LATEST GADGETS, PAPERS AND NEWS.

RASS YIN YANG *(right)*
RASS AND EURO-PAC ARE RELATIVELY NEW PAPERS ON THE SCENE. LIKE SO MANY OTHERS, THEY ORIGINATED IN SPAIN AND ARE EXTREMELY POPULAR AMONGST CULTURED CANNABIS CONNOISSEURS, DUE TO THE FACT THAT MOST OF THEM ARE MADE FROM HEMP.

DIGITAL WEIGHING SCALES *(left)*

WEIGHING YOUR STASH MOVED INTO THE 21ST CENTURY WITH THESE AMAZING TRUWEIGH DIGITAL SCALES THAT MEASURE IN TINY 0.05G INCREMENTS. NOT ONLY THAT, BUT THEY HAVE A SLICK BLUE, BACKLIT DISPLAY FOR WHEN THE LIGHTS ARE DOWN LOW. AVAILABLE IN BLACK OR SILVER, AND IN A HANDY POCKET SIZE, YOU NEED NEVER GET BURNED ON A DEAL AGAIN!

RASTA HEMP PAPER *(right)*

ROLLING PAPERS COME IN A VAST ARRAY OF SHAPES AND FORMS FROM BOOKLETS, COVERS AND BOXES, TO BLOCKS AND ENVELOPES. SIZES CAN RANGE FROM KING SIZE, KING SIZE SLIM, EXTRA LONG, EXTRA WIDE, DOUBLE WIDE, ETC.

RASS RASTER *(left)*

THE RASS RASTER PAPERS COME IN A HANDY WALLET FORMAT, WHICH IS FAR MORE COMMON IN AMERICA THAN IN THE UK OR EUROPE. THEY ARE ALSO IN THE TRADITIONAL REEFER TOKIN' RASTAFARIAN COLOURS OF RED, GOLD AND GREEN.

SMOKING MASTER *(below)*

THE SMOKING BRAND OF PAPERS ARE MADE BY SPANISH GIANT, MIQUEL Y COSTAS & MIQUEL. THE COMPANY WAS FORMED IN 1725 AND STARTED MAKING ROLLING PAPERS IN THE 1820S. THE SMOKING PAPERS WERE LAUNCHED IN 1924 AND ARE NOW SOLD IN OVER 30 COUNTRIES WORLDWIDE.

RIPS WITH ROACH *(right)*

THIS LONG LENGTH RIPS BOX OF PAPER NOT ONLY MEANS THAT YOU CAN ROLL A MASSIVE SPLIFF WITH THE MACHINE BELOW, BUT IT ALSO COMES WITH ITS OWN MATCHING BOOK OF ROACHES FOR THAT CLASSY TOUCH. RIPS INTERNATIONAL LTD IS A UK BASED COMPANY WHO ALSO OPERATE AS AN AGENT FOR MIQUEL Y COSTAS & MIQUEL.

CAMU-FLASH *(below)*

THIS INGENIOUS LITTLE DEVICE, KNOWN AS THE CAMU-FLASH, WILL STRIP OUT THE TOBACCO FROM A REGULAR CIGARETTE AND STUFF IT FULL OF WACKY BACCY! PERFECT FOR STEALTH SMOKING. BUT THE SMELL OF SKUNK MIGHT GIVE YOU AWAY!

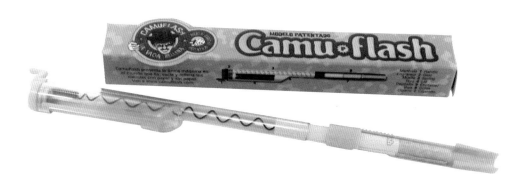

Chapter 8

Medical Marijuana

A potted history of medical marijuana: 2000 BC to the present.

It's no new thing to turn to cannabis for relief from the disease of life. This power packed plant features in the pharmacology of many great dynasties and cultures back to ancient times. It's only in recent years that the herb has been marginalized and/or banned from the heart of modern healing.

Medical marijuana

The earliest reference to cannabis as medicine dates back to the Ancient Egyptian treatment for sore eyes in 2000 BC. Around the Bronze Age (circa 1400 BC), there is evidence in the Mediterranean of a flourishing hashish trade, which supplied, amongst other things, a balm to ease the pain of childbirth. India's doctor/patient relationship with cannabis began way back around 1000 BC when it was, "used… to treat a wide variety of human maladies," according to the US National Commission on Marihuana and Drug Abuse in 1972. Never ones to miss out on a good thing, the Ancient Greeks used cannabis as a remedy for earache, edema and inflammation around 200 BC. At the same time, on the other side of the world, Chinese physician Ho Tho used it as a surgical analgesic. The Roman Emperor Nero's surgeon Dioscorides praised the medical properties of cannabis around 70 BC, and by the time of the birth of Jesus Christ, medical marijuana was being prescribed by switched on doctors from China and India, through to North Africa and all around the Mediterranean.

The first 'modern' recorded use of medical marijuana was in Englishman Robert Burton's book *The Anatomy of Melancholy* published in 1621. Burton saw it as a treatment for depression, but judging by Culpepper's famous herbal tome, the benefits of medicinal hemp were already well established in folk culture by the time he wrote his book of natural remedies in 1653. Culpepper skimmed over the topic casually, "Hemp – this is so well known to every good housewife in the country, that I shall not need to write any description of it." Most notably, the herbalist insisted, "The juice dropped into the ears kills worms in them; and draws forth earwigs, or other living creatures gotten into them." So next time you get bugged, try using a little stash.

The introduction of cannabis to modern Western medicine is attributed to William Brooke O'Shaughnessy, an obscure Irish physician who worked in India where his experiments with the weed began. He returned home with a 'pot-ent' cure all in 1842 and handed over his stash to pharmacist Peter Squire to convert into a form suitable for medical use. The result was Squire's Extract, soon a widely available drug which physicians prescribed for pretty much everything. Queen Victoria's ills were famously treated with dope as prescribed by court physician Dr Reynolds, but whether she allowed herself to

Right: Ancient horticulturalists knew about the holy herb's healing powers.

enjoy the drug's mischievous side effects remains a mystery.

From 1842 to the 1890s, marijuana and hashish extracts stayed in the top three prescribed medicines in the US, with long lists of useful cures for ailments ranging from menstruation to mania, birth pains to bronchitis. But Victorian doctors were already divided about marijuana's place in medicine. While some were sold on its medical effectiveness, others were

Right: Medical marijuana looks clinical on the outside, but is a familiar friend inside.

suspicious of its potential for intoxication; surely something that gets you that wasted can't be good for you, can it? And so a pure extract was sought, with relative success coming in the shape of 'cannabiol' in the 1890s, produced by three Cambridge University chemists. Unfortunately, two of the young scientists were blown to bits whilst working on the project, and a third almost suffered a similar fate. While working in the lab he took some cannabiol and lost consciousness, almost perishing in the ensuing fire.

Suspicions in the medical world grew around the eve of the 20th century, with cannabis eventually outlawed in the UK in 1928 under the Dangerous Drugs Act, and then removed from the US pharmacopoeia in 1941. By 1971, the UK Misuse of Drugs Act attempted to give medical marijuana the final boot, classifying it as a Class B drug, effectively banning the medical use of cannabis. Suddenly the wonder drug prescribed for over 4,000 years in numerous diverse cultures, for a wide range of maladies, became a, "narcotic poison… of doubtful value."

In spite of the increasing vilification of the healing herb, brave and bold researchers continued to illegally explore cannabis' complicated chemistry in the 1980s and 1990s, confirming again and again the claims made by ancient medicine. But opposition remained fierce. Not liking what they heard, the Reagan-

Above: Sir William Brooke O'Shaughnessy, MD, purveyor of fine Indian grasses.

CANNABIS FLOS

variëteit
SIMM 18

5 gram

Ministerie van Volksgezond...
Bureau voor Medicinale Ca...
Den Haag

CANNAB...

variëteit
Bedrocan

5 gram

...rie van Vo...
...a Medic...

Alchemy:
more than just a headshop

Whichever city you are in these days you can be pretty sure you'll find a headshop. These Aladdin's caves of paraphernalia exist to make the smoker's life easier and their highs higher. But it wasn't always like this... Welcome to Alchemy, the UK's first headshop.

In the late Sixties, the world seemed to be on the cusp of something big, a movement of love and peace that would see an end to war and hatred, and the realization that mind altering drugs were not the scourge of society that 'The Man' had said they were. Unfortunately, the movement's time in the limelight was short lived and as the Seventies closed in, thoughts of freedom - in the true sense of the word - were pushed back underground.

For some however, riding high on a tide of long hair and bed protests, the movement provided the starting point for new enterprises. One such man was Lee Harris, owner and original driving force behind Alchemy, the UK's first headshop. Its motto: "Still crazy after all these years". Situated in London's hippest quarter, on Portobello Road, the original idea behind the shop was to sell and give customers access to the blossoming interest in Indian culture and medicine, but Harris' interest in various counterculture movements, plus his experience in publishing and music, meant that Alchemy quickly became *the* place to hang out. Especially if your hair was starting to creep below your collar.

The shop's name came from a 1968 event at the Royal Albert Hall, which Harris helped to organize. John (Lennon) and Yoko (Ono)'s Alchemical Wedding featured music, song, dance and lots of naked people. Well, enough to make the front page of the *London Evening News*. Harris himself had previously sold and made chokers and chillums, touting them at festivals. A shop seemed like the perfect way to gather all his interests together and alert the public to some of the alternative culture happening right under their noses.

Harris' involvement in underground arts saw him launch the cult comic *Brainstorm*, featuring the adventures of psychedelic alchemist Chester P Hackenbush. He was also the man behind Europe's first cannabis magazine, *Homegrown*, which first rolled off the presses in 1977. Such exploits brought him into contact with many of the luminaries of the day, including LSD pioneer Timothy Leary and American poet Alan Ginsberg.

Harris was also an advocate of cannabis, attending rallies ever since the day he got busted and fined for possession. By the time he was busted again in 1989, for selling king size rolling

Right: Alchemy, on Portobello Road in Notting Hill, London.

207

Above: Lee Harris – publisher, founder of Alchemy, and lovely bloke.

papers at Alchemy, his almost celebrity status secured him enough headlines to guarantee only one night in a cell. However, Harris' relationship with cannabis goes further than the odd toke on a doobie. He's a firm believer in its medicinal value and its reputation as the healing herb.

Selling papers isn't such an issue anymore and Alchemy now boasts an extensive selection of skins, along with classic pipes from around the world. It is also a visionary in pipe smoking technology, being the first to sell the famous Silver Palm Leaf pipe, and now championing America's Protopipe. Smoking paraphernalia aside, Alchemy stocks cultural t-shirts, comics, Jamaican music producer Lee 'Scratch' Perry's *The Upsetter* magazine and all sorts of Rastafarian products. Stocking a wide range of books and magazines, it is also the place to go if you are interested in the issues surrounding cannabis, its culture, history or use as cloth, paper, oil and food.

In 2002, Alchemy celebrated its 30th anniversary by releasing a commemorative CD which has recently been re-released. *Alchemy – 30 Years of Counter Culture* features an eclectic mix of fusion, dub, ambient trance, jazz and spoken word from a wealth of cultural rebels; Howard Marks, Raja Ram, Simon Posford, Drum Druids and Bush Chemist. Drezz, of Nervasystem, one of the musicians involved with the album, remembers the experience, "Most of the artists involved are regular visitors to the most classic of headshops, Alchemy, which seems to be, along with its proprietor, a catalyst for synchronistic creativities. All the heads, beautiful people, shakers, takers, brain benders & menders, gurus, Rastas, ascended masters, travellers, seers, starseed extraterrestrials, and whatever else lives and breathes in London seems to find its way to that colourful emporium of all things alchemical."

If you count yourself among that community, you owe it to yourself to discover London's centre for all things alternative. So, next time you're in Britain's capital city, take the Hammersmith & City Line underground to Ladbroke Grove, head over to 261 Portobello Road and check out a part of herbal history.

Right: Alchemy is more than a head shop; it's a countercultural epicentre.

Bush administration proposed destroying all of the 1966-1976 cannabis research work and libraries – an idea which luckily went up in smoke, unlike the research. In the late 1990s, President Clinton even proposed to take criminal proceedings against physicians who prescribed or recommended marijuana. This, coming from the President who, "didn't inhale" marijuana at university and definitely, "did not have sexual relations with that woman, Monica Lewinsky." Take a chill pill, Bill.

However, since the dawn of the new Millennium things have begun to look up. There is a growing acceptance of marijuana's medical potential, though it still remains illegal to buy the drug. By the end of 2004, medical marijuana was legal in 11 US States, enabling people with AIDS, cancer and glaucoma to legally grow and smoke it. However, for those without green fingers, buying your medical stash remains a problem which is difficult to solve.

Surprisingly, until 1971 it was still possible to pop into a UK chemist's to pick up your prescription cannabis. Since then, most patients have been forced to buy their medicine on the black market. There are several suppliers of medical quality cannabis in the UK, many of them, such as THC4MS, receiving donations of weed from growers and re-distributing it to bona fide patients. Others, such as Tony's Holistic Centre in London, sell cannabis products to patients who have a qualifying condition or a GP referral. Unfortunately, police raids are still a periodic risk.

The situation is pretty similar across the Atlantic. In the USA, unless you are one of the seven patients being supplied with medi-marijuana under the Compassionate Investigative New Drugs programme, you cannot as yet legally

buy your medicine of choice in the US. Raids of medical cannabis co-ops are a real and regular risk. A typical example of heavy handed 'justice' was the trial of Californian Brian Epis in 2002, when the jury was instructed to, "disregard

Above: Rosie Boycott (centre, standing), the then editor of *The Independent on Sunday*, helps a medical marijuana user at the decriminalization rally in 1997.

"We don't see evidence of high psychological disturbance among the [long term users]... The results seem unremarkable; the exceptional thing is that the respondents are unexceptional."

Chief Investigator David Reilly, National Drug and Alcohol Research Centre in Australia, 20 March 1997.

"We... say that on the medical evidence available, moderate indulgence in cannabis has little ill effect on health, and that decisions to ban or legalize cannabis should be based on other considerations."

The Lancet, volume 352, number 9140, 14 November 1998.

medicinal use evidence and argument." Epis was sentenced to a staggering 10 years in jail for growing marijuana medicine, but was released pending appeal in 2004.

Yet America's nearest neighbour, Canada, has seen the light. Medical marijuana was legalized in July 2001, but the terminally ill and those with AIDS, arthritis and cancer are expected to grow their own supply, or at least get a mate to do it for them. By the time the forms have been signed by your doctor and two other experts, you've had a crash course in cannabis cultivation and have finally grown a decent crop, the grim reaper may have already popped by for a visit. Government concessions were made in 2003 when 10 patients received cannabis from the administration, though the authorities clearly need to refine their hydroponics – "disgusting" one patient complained, while another dismissed it as, "totally unfit for human consumption." Yet another described the government grass as "Shwag", the lowest grade weed that, "wouldn't hold a candle to street level cannabis."

As always, it took the progressive Dutch to come up with another international first when, in September 2001, the government in Holland set up the world's first medical marijuana programme. Since 2003, all Dutch pharmacies have had to dish out medi-marijuana and sing its praises. But against all odds, the Dutch government has been left with rather a lot of pot on their hands. Of the 10,000-15,000 cannabis patients in Holland, only about 10% go to the pharmacies, leaving the Dutch government with surpluses of up to 330kgs of unused grass. Why? Maybe it's because it costs twice as much as the coffee shops (€9 per gram as opposed to €4-€5), or maybe it's because Dutch medi-marijuana is designed to be a steam inhalation treatment or a tea. There's just nothing quite like a spliff.

Medical properties and active chemical components

Tod Mikuriya MD, one of the world's leading authorities on medical marijuana, cites 222 medical conditions reported to be helped by using cannabis. Of the 60+ phytocannabinoids in weed, medical research has primarily focused on two: THC and CBD. THC is said have the following medical properties – *analgesic, anti-spasmodic, anti-tremor, anti-inflammatory, anti-emetic (stops nausea and vomiting) and appetite-stimulant.* CBD is said to be *anti-inflammatory, anti-convulsant, anti-psychotic and anti-oxidant.* Both are soporific and aid sleep. Below are some of the most widely documented medical conditions supposedly helped by marijuana.

AIDS: Cannabis is said to support patients with nausea, anxiety, pain and in appetite stimulation. Whilst some doctors have argued that THC can reduce the effectiveness of the immune system's T-cells, more recnt studies have been unable to

Right: Canadian prescription cannabis is dispensed in clinical conditions.

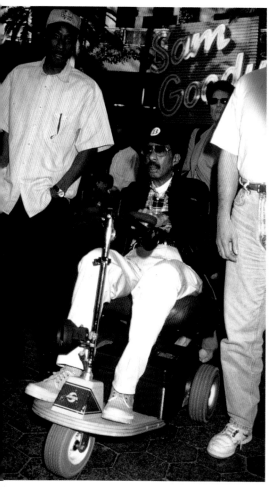

find supporting evidence, and in 1992 the Food and Drug Administration officially approved the use of synthetic THC (Marinol) in the treatment of AIDS wasting syndrome. GW Pharmaceuticals notes that, "Presently, medical organizations specializing in AIDS research are some of the strongest advocates for legalizing medical cannabis, calling it 'potentially life saving medicine'."

Cancer: It's now widely accepted that marijuana can help reduce the side effects of chemotherapy, especially nausea. Patients administered oral THC experienced a 76-88% reduction in symptoms of nausea and vomiting, whilst spliffs gave 70-100% relief. One American breast cancer victim wrote a letter to the *LA Times* stating, "Marijuana was a miracle drug for me. [It was] the only thing that kept me symptom free." Another patient, a 52 year old man with non-Hodgkin's Lymphoma could only get one hour's shut eye on top strength sleeping medication. However, two tokes on a bedtime spliff inspired seven hours' sleep, "If I hadn't gotten the rest and had not been able to eat, I'd be dead," he said.

Chronic pain: Again and again, in a wide array of illnesses, patients celebrate cannabis' pain relieving properties. It helps with nerve pain

Left: Comedian Richard Pryor is a vocal campaigner for decriminalization.

and even phantom limb pain and works in cases where traditional opiates fail. One man with a painful degenerative disease, shared his experience with *The LA Times* in 2003, "Unless I can smoke or eat pot, I am in excruciating pain from morning to night… Given the pain relief provided by marijuana, I am able to bicycle great distances." Perhaps George W Bush and his fellow prohibitionists should get on their bikes.

Multiple Sclerosis: "MS is one of the most frequent reasons that patients employ cannabis,"

Above: Author, campaigner and legend, Ed Rosenthal in 2003, outside a San Francisco court just before he was convicted of supplying medical marijuana.

according to a GW report in 2004, and top officials on both sides of the Atlantic have the proof to back this up. Although there appears to be strong variability between doses needed to produce an effect, get it right and very real clinical improvement is possible, "In some cases, improvements have been sufficient to transform lives." One life transformed by using dope for his MS is that of US chat show host Montel Williams, who suffered nerve pain 24 hours a day. In his book *Climbing Higher*, the former anti-drug spokesperson rails against a medical system that prescribes addictive painkillers but not marijuana, "Why? Because we have an idea that everybody who does it sits around smoking." In fact, most MS suffers who use marijuana want to stop sitting around and get back out there.

You don't have to smoke it

Medical marijuana can be administered in several ways, other than smoking, although for the pothead who becomes ill, this is the most obvious way. It provides a quick fix in an easily controlled manner, but, although research to date has proved inconclusive, there is evidence to suggest that smoking cannabis leads to an increased risk of pulmonary infections and respiratory cancers. Smoking is only a viable option in the short term as Joycelyn Elders MD, the former US Surgeon General, noted in 2004, "For many who need only a small amount – such as cancer patients trying to get through a few months of chemotherapy – the risks of smoking are minor." For longer marijuana programmes however, it's worth looking at other options.

Right: American talk show host, Montel Williams uses medical marijuana to ease the pain from his Multiple Sclerosis.

Vaporizing – or phytoinhalation, if you are posh – is reputedly the cleanest way of inhaling cannabis. Grass or hash is heated to temperatures of 130°-230°, releasing THC without burning it, and without the toxins which come rolled in a spliff. Good vaporizers are effective within a minute and allow good dose control and are useful for most symptoms and conditions. But it can be hard to get the temperature right and results fade after one or two hours.

Cannabis chocolate is a safe, easy and tasty way for non-smokers to benefit from the medical advantages of weed. Three squares a day is the average dose recommended by THC4MS, UK producers of medi-chocolate for MS, which contains about 2% raw cannabis. A note of caution for those whose intentions are pure though. San Diego neuroscientists have finally acknowledged what brownie eaters have known for years; that the anandamine in chocolate prolongs and intensifies the THC high. In medical lingo, the undesirable psychoactive side effects are exacerbated!

Tablets & sprays are currently being developed by GW under a special Home Office Licence (1998) and should be prescription medicines in the next few years. Clinical trials are almost complete with the end product, Sativex, ready to roll out. It promises pain relief with a minimal high and is easily dissolved or sprayed under the tongue for tight dosage control. It has been warmly welcomed by many charities including Arthritis Research Campaign, who are keen to see a cannabis drug which moves away from the stereotype of patients, "sitting around smoking joints and getting high."

Tincture – A traditional form of herbal remedy, a tincture is useful for on the go medication favoured by pain patients. Cannabis flowers and leaves are steeped in alcohol, which becomes infused with THC and other cannabinoids. A few drops of the tincture under the tongue will enter the blood stream in minutes or, added to food or drink will take about half an hour. Drop by drop administration is perfect for the patient who wants tight control over dosage and is reluctant to end up high. Nevertheless, its main drawback is that it is too weak a remedy for some.

Essential oil – It's no mean feat extracting a volatile essence from a plant, especially when you are seriously ill. Steam distillation equipment is needed, and you must get the temperature, time and pressure spot on. All very complicated unless you have that bio-chemistry degree, but useful if you get there, as you end up with a very versatile drug which can be inhaled using a vaporizer, directly added to foods or liquids, or else applied to the skin in massage oil. Not for those on a budget; less than one gram of oil is produced from each ounce of leaf, and one to three grams from one ounce of bud. A designer drug for the aromatherapy clique.

Butters – The budding kitchen chemist can simmer your best stash in butter or vegetable oil for several hours until it is a good, dark green and full of THC. Bin the bud and your remedy is ready to add to brownies, cakes and savoury dishes. Results last for several hours so it's good for overnight pain relief, but can take 30-90 minutes to kick in. It's also hard to get the dose right and it's too late if you haven't. The effects increase for hours after eating, but can give the best sustained pain relief once you know how much to use. However, butters is not, perhaps, the best choice if your marijuana programme is designed to counteract nausea, vomiting or loss of appetite; standing and stirring a heaving pot of green grease is unlikely to appeal to most of us, let alone those seeking therapy for a weak stomach.

Ointments – These can be bought from some of the medical marijuana dispensaries, but you can easily make your own at home. Take 100mls of the above goo and add 1g of beeswax. Melt slowly, pour into an airtight jar and allow it to cool. It will solidify into a useful ointment for rubbing into aching joints and frayed nerves.

Be safe

Marijuana is a famously safe, non-physically addictive drug with no known fatalities linked to overdose and a, "very limited toxicity." A study by GW in 2001 found that they didn't need to increase patients' dosages over time as no tolerance to the active ingredient was reported. However, as any stoner will tell you, the more you smoke, the more you'll *need* to smoke to get high, as tolerance builds to the 'high' factor of THC. Before launching into any experiments with marijuana as medicine, explore. There are plenty of web sites and organizations out there to guide users. Here are a few final pointers for a journey to better health:

Find a dope doctor – There are an increasing number of cannabis friendly practices out there which will support patients with those major diseases which research has shown can be helped with weed. These include AIDS, cancer, MS, arthritis, glaucoma, nerve disorders, and chronic pain amongst others.

Don't lose your marbles – Check out the risks linked to long term or heavy marijuana intake before you embark. Impairment in brain function, memory loss, depression, attention problems and lowered IQ in heavy users have all been documented. Epilepsy and schizophrenia can both be triggered by dope.

Breathe easy – Look at the alternatives to smoking if you're going for optimum health. According to the British Lung Foundation's 2002 report, three or four cannabis cigarettes are as harmful to the lungs as around 20 tobacco cigarettes.

Dose the dope – Fine tune your medicine so you get the benefits without getting too spun out. Find the purest weed you can and if you are not with a medi-marijuana supplier, be prepared for fluctuations in strength and quality.

Look to the future – With the government finally approving research into medical marijuana, it looks like cannabis based medicines may well be in UK pharmacies in the next few years. Whether these will be as effective as a good bit of home grown remains to be seen, but one thing is for sure, it will be more expensive. Harvard psychiatrist Lester Grinspoon predicts, "We can anticipate two medical distribution networks; a legal one for cannabinoid pharmaceuticals and an illegal one for street or home grown marijuana." But for the time being, the vision of buying a month's supply of marijuana medicine from your local herbalist without the risk of persecution remains a pipe dream.

Right: While little scientific research has been done on cannabis, one company, GW Pharmaceuticals, has released a cannabis-derived pain killer called Sativex® in Canada.

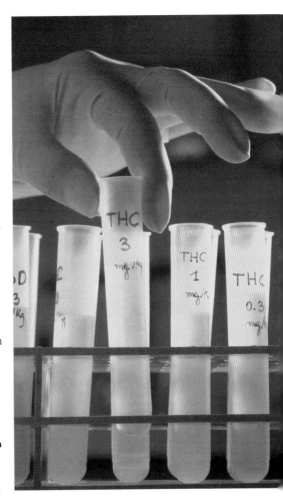

Further reading

Barret, Leonard E Senior: *The Rastafarians*,
Boston, Beacon Press, 1997

Boon, Marcus: *The Road Of Excess*, Harvard
University Press, 2002

Clarke, Robert C: *Hashish!*, Red Eye Press,
California,1998

Davenport-Hines, Richard: *The Pursuit of
Oblivion*, London, Weidenfeld & Nicolson, 2000

Frank, Mel: *Marijuana Grower's Inside Guide*,
California, Red Eye Press, 1988

Green, Jonathon: *Cannabis*,
London, Pavilion, 2002

Herer, Jack: *The Emperor Wears No Clothes*,
Quick American Archives, 1979

Jones, Nick: *Spliffs*
London, Chrysalis Books, 2003

King, Jason: *The Cannabible*, California,
Ten Speed Press, 2001

Ludlow, Fitzhugh: *The Hasheesh Eater*,
New York, Harper and Brothers, 1857
Marks, Howard: *Mr Nice*,
London, Secker & Warburg, 1996

Marks, Howard: *The Howard Marks Book of
Dope Stories*, London, Vintage, 2001

Matthews, Patrick: *Cannabis Culture*,
London, Bloomsbury, 1999

Mezzrow, Milton & Wolfe Bernard: *Really
The Blues*, New York, Random House, 1946

Preston, Brian: *Pot Planet: Adventures in
Global Marijuana Culture*,
Grove Press, 2002

Rosenthal, Ed: *Marijuana Growers Handbook*,
California, Quick American Publishing Company,
1984

Shapiro, Harry: *Waiting For The Man*,
London, Mandarin, 1990

Sloman, Larry: *Reefer Madness: The History of
Marijuana in America*, New York,
Bobbs-Merrill, 1979

Solomon, David: *The Marihuana Papers*,
New York, Bobbs-Merrill, 1966

Watts, Alan W: *The Joyous Cosmology*,
New York, Random House, 1965

Pilcher, Tim: *Spliffs 2*, London,
Chrysalis Books, 2004

Wishnia, Steven: *The Cannabis Companion*
Hoo, Grange Books, 2004

Stevenson, Jack: *Addicted: The Myth and
Menace of Drugs in Film*
New York, Creations Books, 2000

Acknowledgements

Wow, what a year and a response from the last book! Thank you to everyone for their continued support and praise. First and foremost, thanks has to go to my fantastic team – Michelle Guilford and Rob Tribe – who once again ably assisted me with reefer research and wonderful writing. Again the whole team at EDIT (Everybodydoesit.com) and the guys at *Cannabis Culture* Magazine for the pics and Alan Lighfoot for the use of his rolling paper collection, cheers fellas! Thanks to David "Cheeky" Bramwell for letting me wax lyrical on cannabis conspiracies at his excellent Catalyst Club in Brighton. Thanks also to Andrew Bennett, Roy Daley, Rhona Ford, Annemarie Carr and everyone at HIT for inviting me to 2nd Perspectives on Cannabis Conference and for looking after me so well. A big shout to the people I met there, like Derek Williams from UKCIA, and fellow speakers Niall Coggins, Paul Dillon (thanks for the Aussie leads!), Dr Amanda Amos, and my train-buddy Dr Zerrin Atakan who all made positive impressions with their differing, but equally valid points of view. Thanks to Chris Stone at Chrysalis for all your faith, patience and commissions. Keep 'em coming! This one's for all pioneers like Lee Harris at Alchemy, Gilbert Shelton and everyone else I've been lucky to meet. It's also for the stoners I know, and I'm not naming anyone this time. And of course the ubiquitous thanks to my wonderful family, who despite their seemingly endless patience are actually very glad this book's over. And that includes Molly.

Picture credits

Chrysalis Books Group Plc is committed to respecting the intellectual property rights of others. We have therefore taken all reasonable efforts to ensure that the reproduction of all content on these pages is done with the full consent of copyright owners. If you are aware of any unintentional omissions please contact the company directly so that any necessary corrections may be made for future editions.

The Advertising Archives: 111, 112; Alamy Images: Edward Parker 81; David Hoffman Photo Library 83, 95, 210-211; Rob Walls 87; Jaime Marshall 102; Courtesy of www.althealthsys.net: 204; Bridgeman Art Library: Self portrait under the Influence of Harschisch, C.1844 (w/c on paper), Baudelaire, Charles Pierre (1821-67) / Bibliotheque Nationale, Paris, France, Archives Charmet. 25, Drawing produced under the influence of hashish (pen & ink on paper), charcot, Jean-Martin (1825-93)/Hopital de la Salpetriere Paris, France, Archives Charmet. 26-27; www.cannabisculture.com: 167, 169-171, 179, 184, 185, 188, 189 TL, 189 R; Chrysalis Image Library: 206-209; Neil Sutherland FC, FC S, 1, 3; Phil Clucas 7, 14, 15, 18, 19, 36, 48, 56, 57, 106, 116, 117, 136, 158, 159, 190, 200; Corbis: Daniel Lainé 12; Earl & Nazima Kowall 28; Bettmann 39, 41, 63, 203; Wally McNamee 64; Gideon Mendel 68; Adrian Arbib 73; Henry Diltz 96T, 140, 156, 161T; Lee Snider/Photo Images 96B; David Pollack 115; Jeffrey L. Rotman 139, 141, 191; Russell Underwood 145; The Cover Story 153; Tim Page 154, 155; Reuters 217; Corbis SYGMA: Alain Nogues 35; Rune Helleestad 67; Gregory Pace 93; Cedric Arnold 160; Everyonedoesit.com: 178, 192 to 199; Empics: DPA Deutsche Press-Agentur 177;

Everynight Images: Debbie Bragg 16; Getty Images: Eric Meola 22; Peter Adams 23; Yann Layma 32; John Lund 97; Keren Su 105; High Times: Trans-High Corp/High Times Archive 172, 173 175TL, 175 TR, 175 BR; Impact Photos: Colin Jones 13, 20; Courtesy of www.jackherer.com: 129, 131; The Kobal Collection: Tony Costa 107; Warner Bros./ First National 109; Warner Bros. 118, 119; Paramount 120-121; Columbia 125; Laurence Cherniak 144C; Mirrorpix: 47; Marijuana Policy Project: 59; NORML Foundation: 48-49; Photolibrary.com: Strand Hans 9; Ariadne Van Zandbergen 11; Planetary Pride: 144TL, 144CL, 144BL, 144TR, 144CR, 144BR; PowerStock/ Superstock Ltd: Michler 84; Gary Pearl 91; Rex Features: Y Tzur/Israel Sun 2; MXL 29; Roger-Viollet 30-31, 79; Nils Jorgensen 37; Julian Makey 43; MAI 44, 45; Sipa Press 53, 60, 99, 136, 162; Charles Sykes 54; Dean Picture 74; Philippe Hays 77; Everett Collection 127, 132; Tim Rooke 134-135; Philip Moore 147; Peter Brooker 149; ISOPress Senepart 151; SWS 165; Ray Tang 176; Dan Tuffs 181; Rozenn Leboucher 182-183; Eric Vidal 201, 205, 215; ADC 216; Stewart Cooke 218; Science Photo Library: Dave Reede/AGSTOCK 80; Mauro Fermariello 221; Stephen Bossonet 161BR; Werner Forman Archive: Provincial Museum, Victoria, British Columbia 33; Museum of American Indian, Heye Foundation, New York 34; Zefa Visual Media UK Ltd: Jeremy Maude/Masterfile 17